SUPERMAN® FAMILY ADVENTURES™

STONE ARCH BOOKS
a capstone imprint

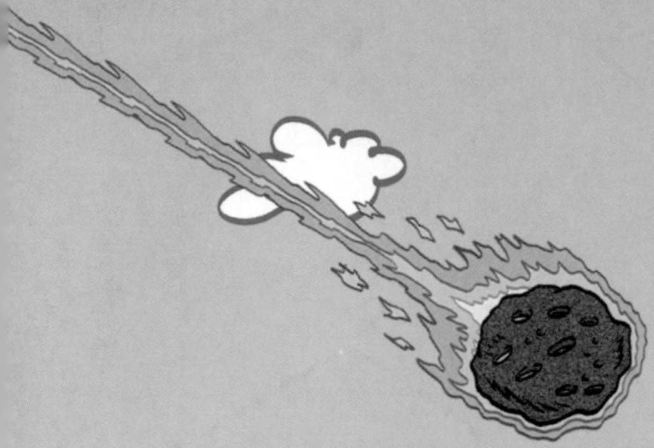

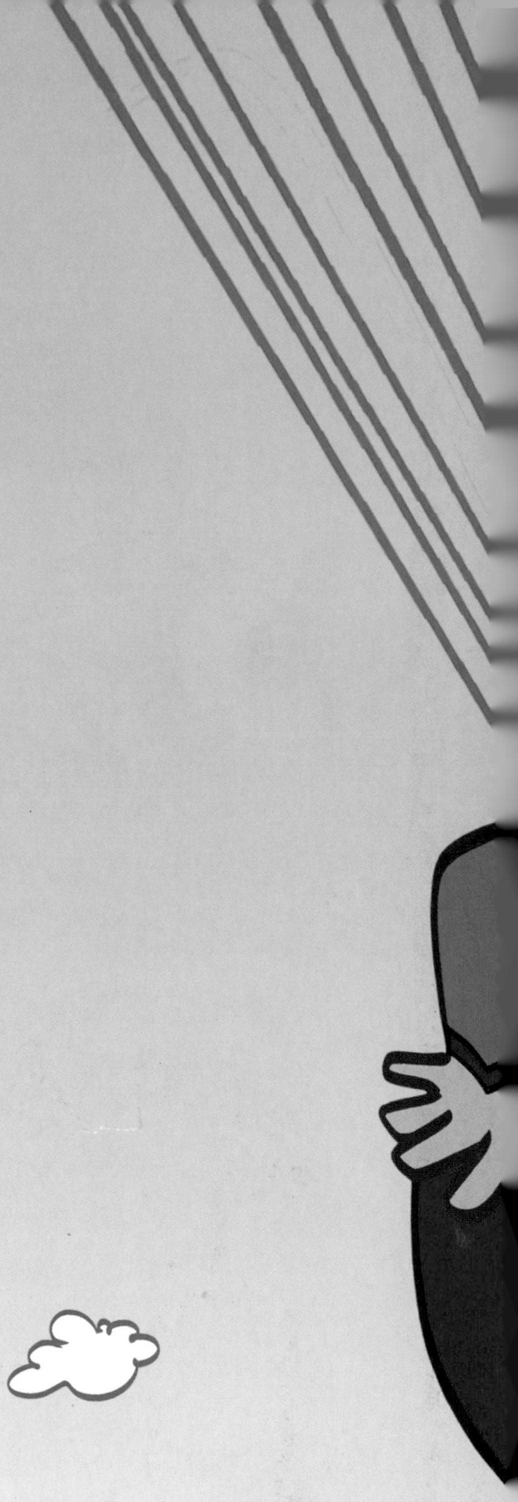

STONE ARCH BOOKS™

Published in 2013
A Capstone Imprint
1710 Roe Crest Drive
North Mankato, MN 56003
www.capstonepub.com

Originally published by DC Comics in the U.S. in single magazine form as SUPERMAN FAMILY ADVENTURES #2.

DC Comics
1700 Broadway, New York, NY 10019
A Warner Bros. Entertainment Company

Cataloging-in-Publication Data is available at the Library of Congress website:
ISBN: 978-1-4342-4790-2 (library binding)

Summary: Superman trains his young sidekicks to become Super Heroes! Bizarro comes to Earth and makes a mess of Metropolis! Jimmy Olsen finds out that being Supermans pal means help is only a shout away!!

STONE ARCH BOOKS
Ashley C. Andersen Zantop Publisher
Michael Dahl Editorial Director
Donald Lemke Editor
Brann Garvey Designer
Kathy McColley Production Specialist

DC COMICS
Kristy Quinn Original U.S. Editor

Printed in China by Nordica.
0413/CA21300442
032013 007226NORDF13

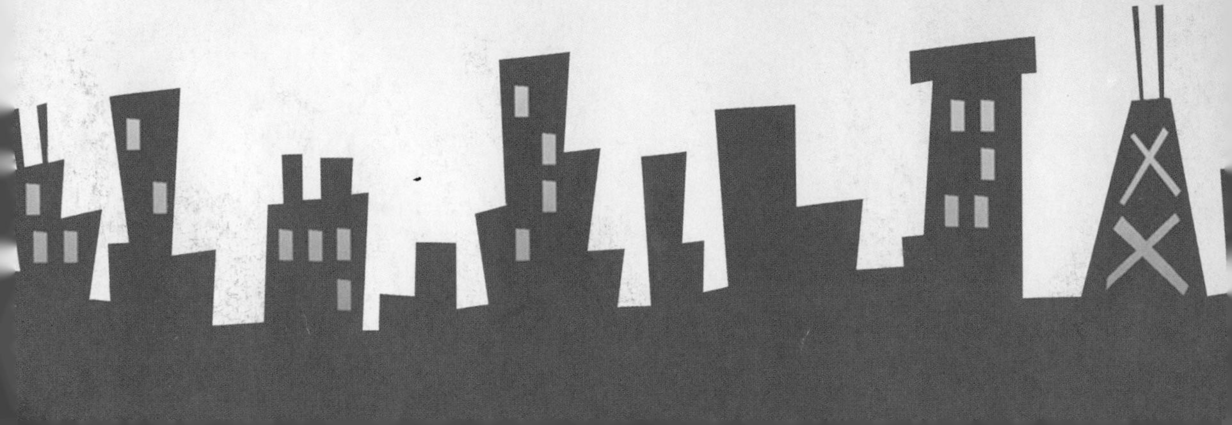

SUPERMAN® FAMILY ADVENTURES™

ENTER BIZARRO!

by Art Baltazar & Franco

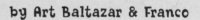

SUPERMAN® FAMILY ADVENTURES™

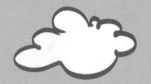

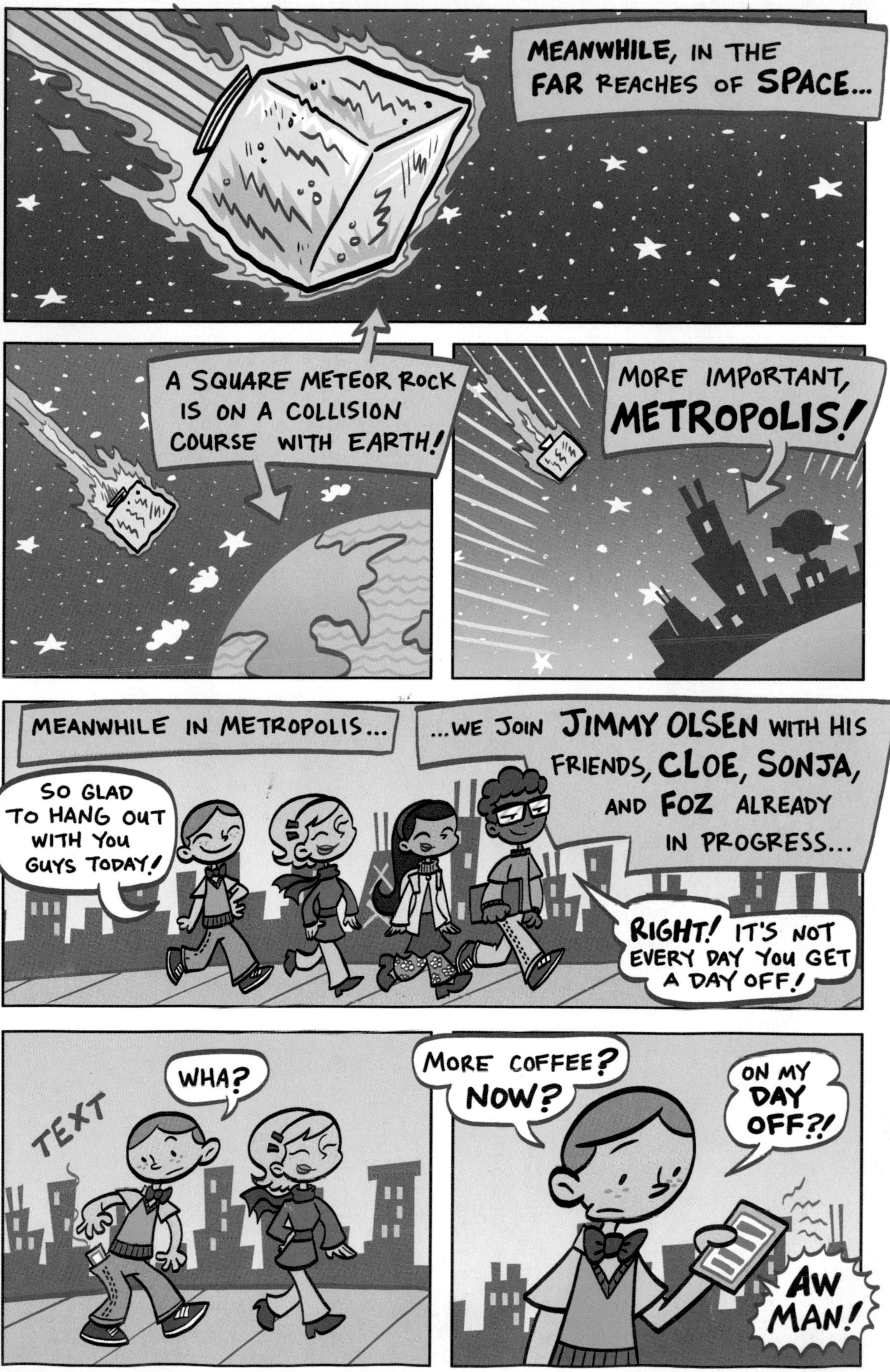
MEANWHILE, IN THE FAR REACHES OF SPACE...
A SQUARE METEOR ROCK IS ON A COLLISION COURSE WITH EARTH!
MORE IMPORTANT, METROPOLIS!
MEANWHILE IN METROPOLIS...
...WE JOIN JIMMY OLSEN WITH HIS FRIENDS, CLOE, SONJA, AND FOZ ALREADY IN PROGRESS...
SO GLAD TO HANG OUT WITH YOU GUYS TODAY!
RIGHT! IT'S NOT EVERY DAY YOU GET A DAY OFF!
TEXT
WHA?
MORE COFFEE? NOW?
ON MY DAY OFF?!
AW MAN!

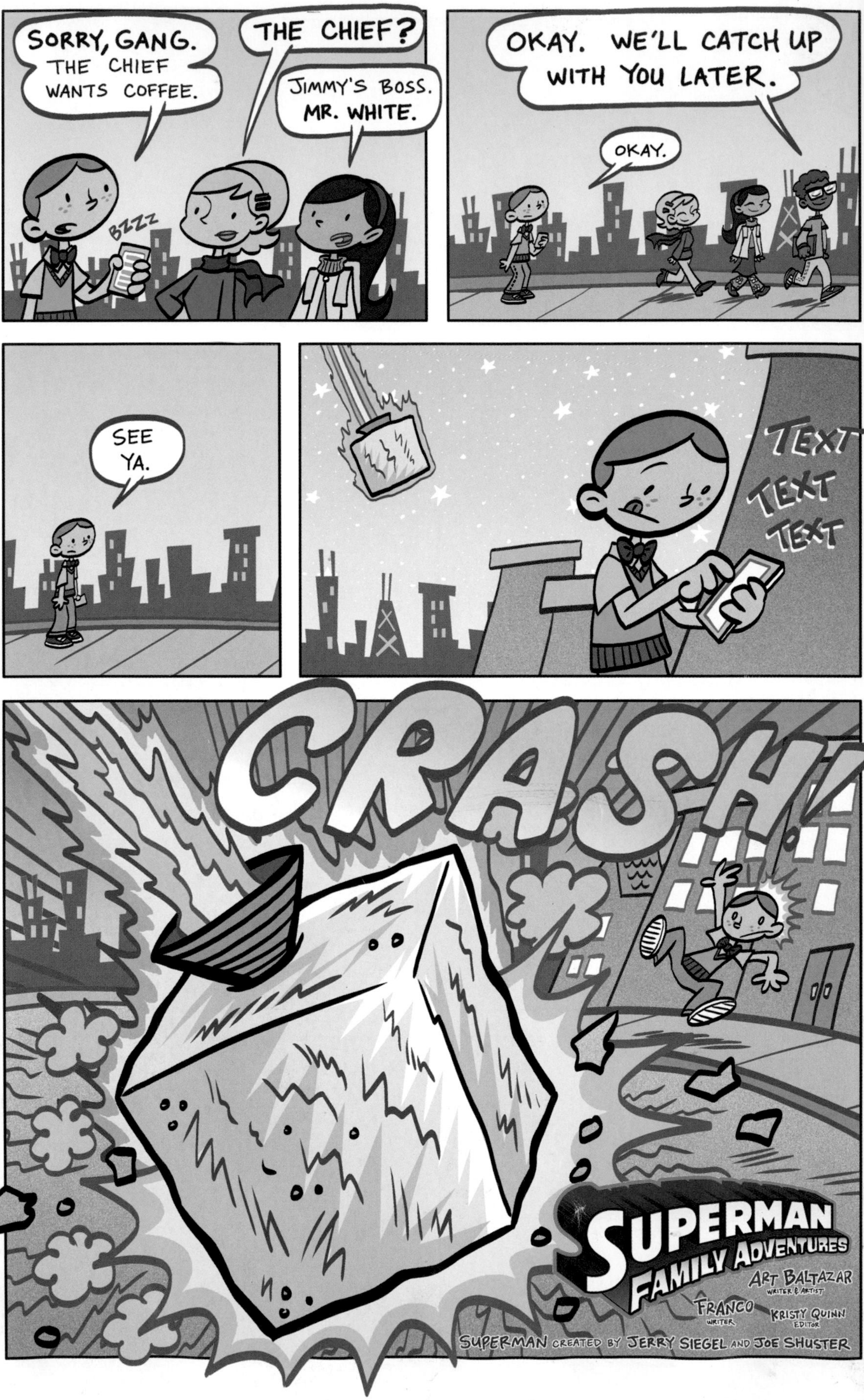
SORRY, GANG. THE CHIEF WANTS COFFEE.
BZZZ
THE CHIEF?
JIMMY'S BOSS. MR. WHITE.
OKAY. WE'LL CATCH UP WITH YOU LATER.
OKAY.
SEE YA.
TEXT TEXT TEXT
CRASH!
SUPERMAN FAMILY ADVENTURES
ART BALTAZAR WRITER & ARTIST
FRANCO WRITER
KRISTY QUINN EDITOR
SUPERMAN CREATED BY JERRY SIEGEL AND JOE SHUSTER

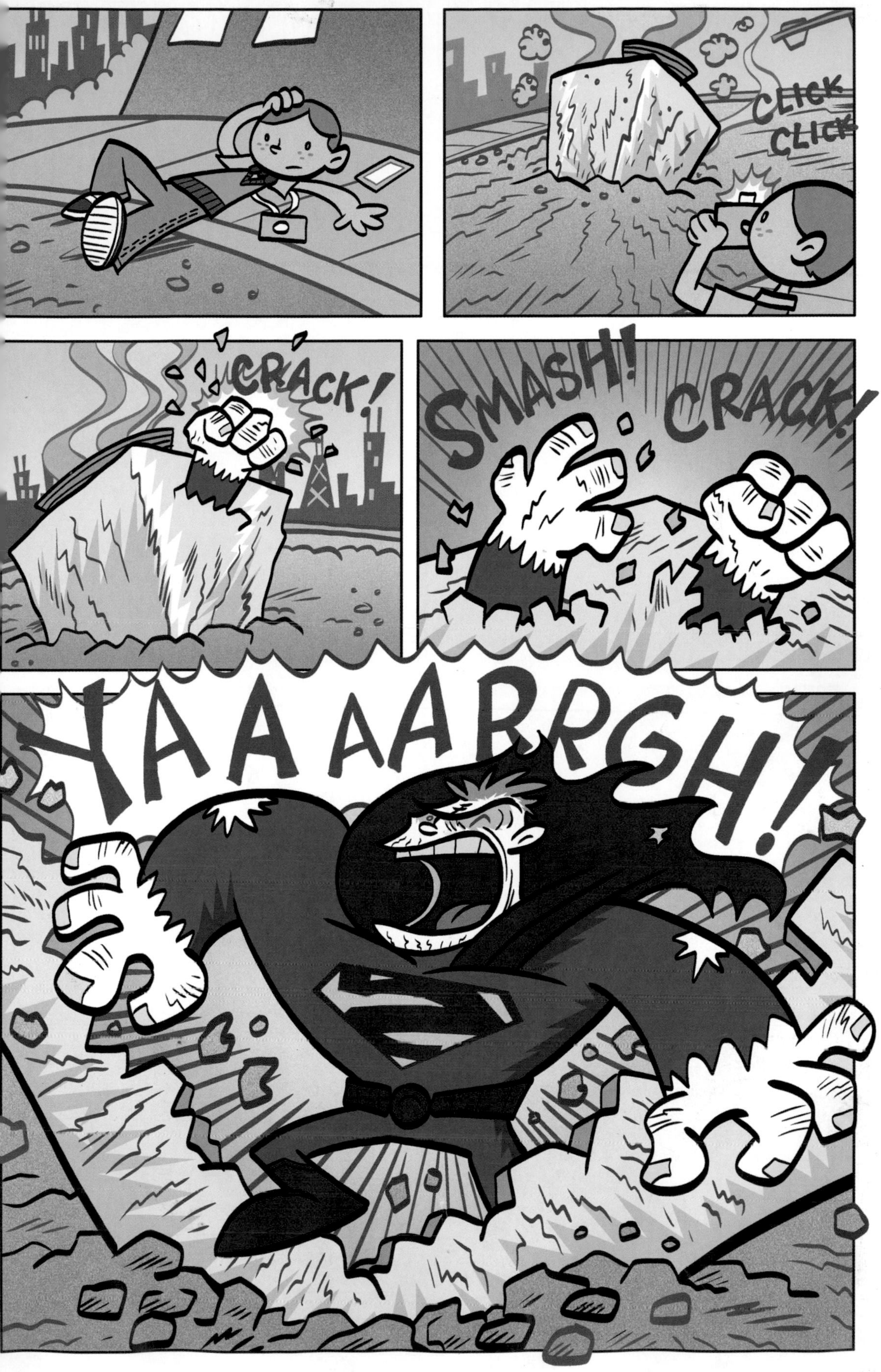
CLICK
CLICK
CRACK!
SMASH!
CRACK!
YAAAARRGH!

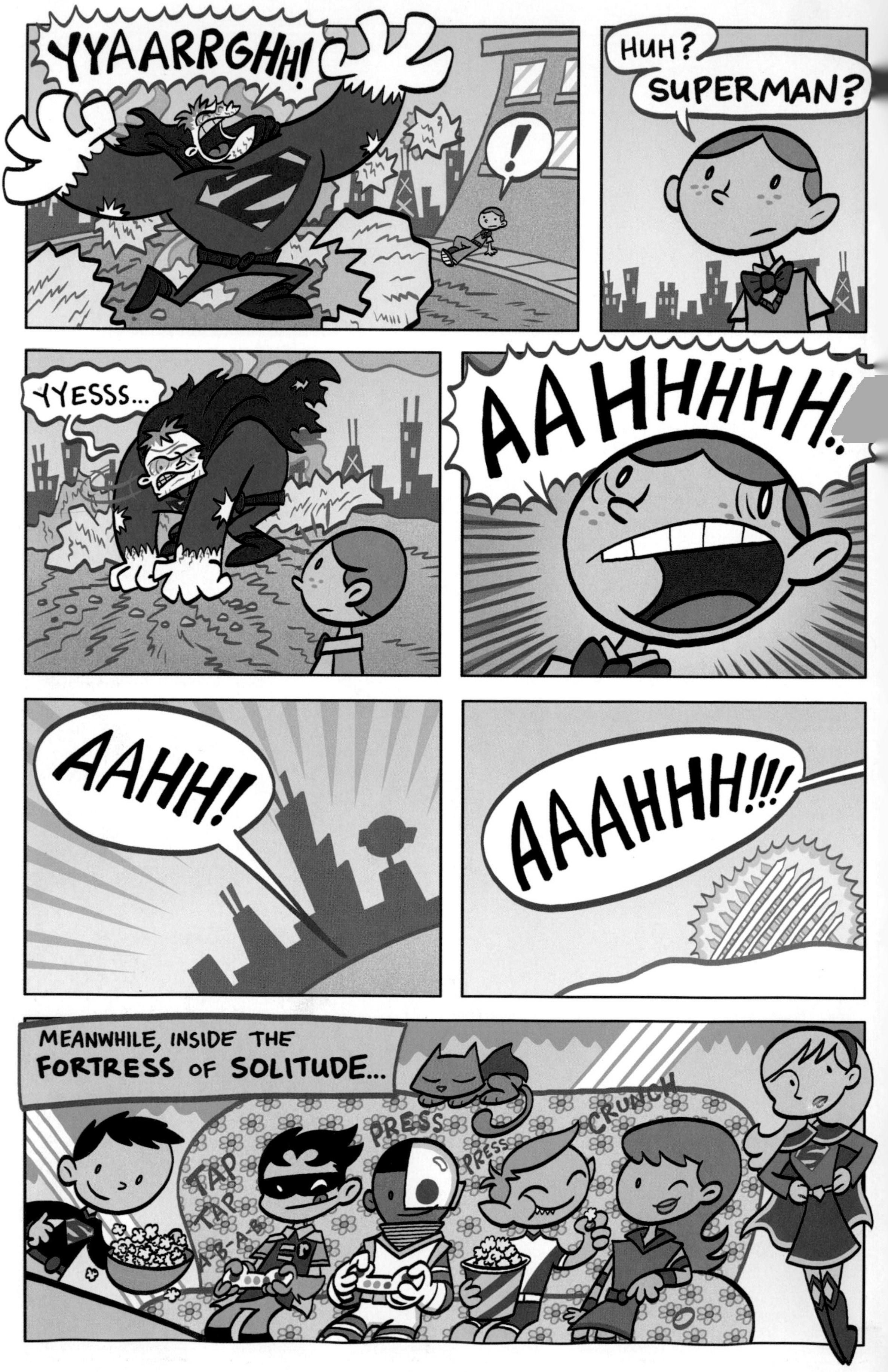
YYAARRGHH!
!
HUH? SUPERMAN?
YYESSS...
AAHHHHH...
AAHH!
AAAHHH!!!
MEANWHILE, INSIDE THE FORTRESS OF SOLITUDE...
TAP TAP
A-B-A-B
PRESS
PRESS
CRUNCH

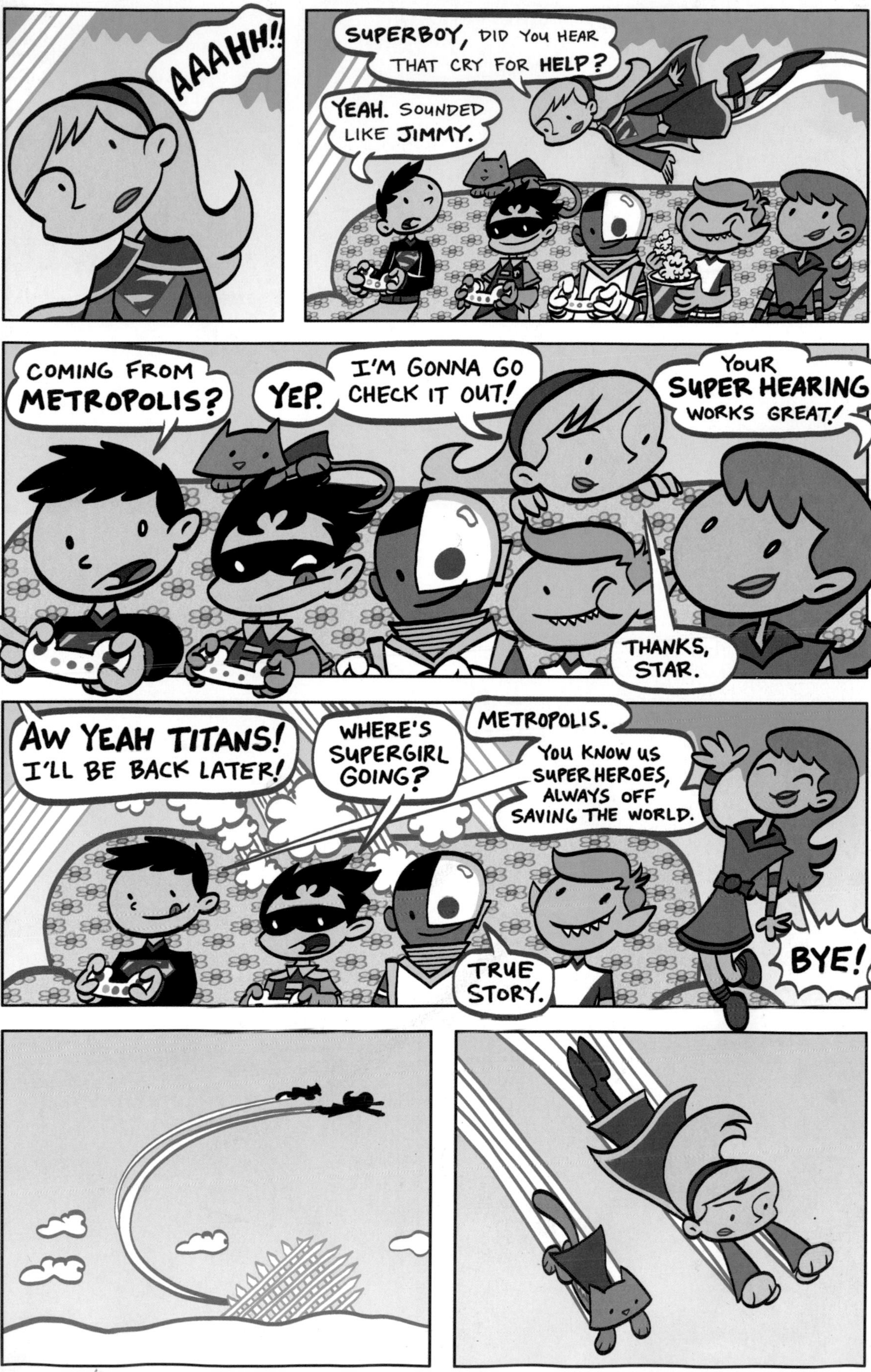
AAAHH!!
SUPERBOY, DID YOU HEAR THAT CRY FOR HELP?
YEAH. SOUNDED LIKE JIMMY.
COMING FROM METROPOLIS?
YEP.
I'M GONNA GO CHECK IT OUT!
YOUR SUPER HEARING WORKS GREAT!
THANKS, STAR.
AW YEAH TITANS! I'LL BE BACK LATER!
WHERE'S SUPERGIRL GOING?
METROPOLIS.
YOU KNOW US SUPERHEROES, ALWAYS OFF SAVING THE WORLD.
TRUE STORY.
BYE!

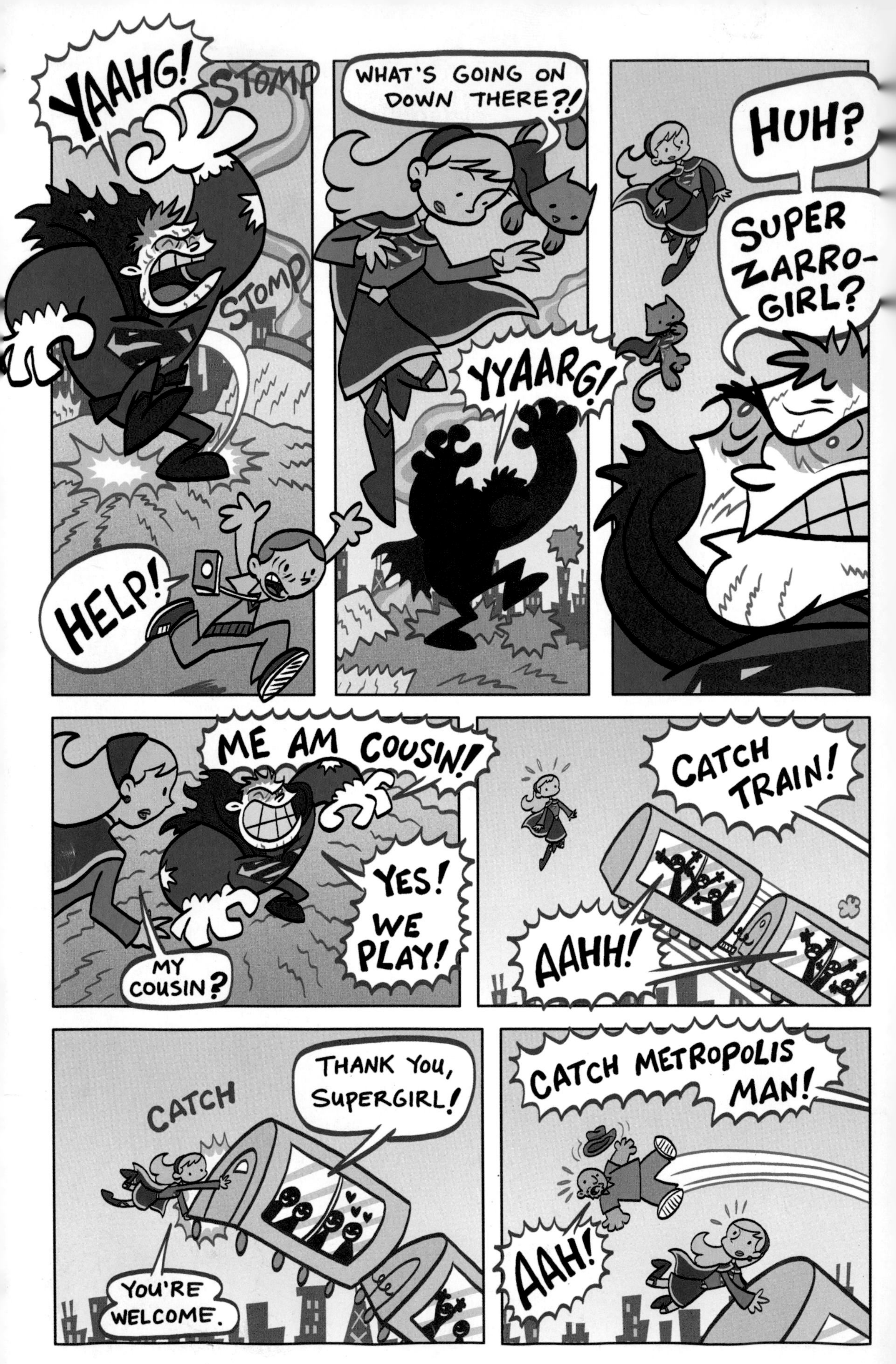
YAAHG!
STOMP
STOMP
HELP!
WHAT'S GOING ON DOWN THERE?!
YYAARG!
HUH?
SUPER ZARRO-GIRL?
ME AM COUSIN!
MY COUSIN?
YES! WE PLAY!
CATCH TRAIN!
AAHH!
CATCH
THANK YOU, SUPERGIRL!
YOU'RE WELCOME.
CATCH METROPOLIS MAN!
AAH!

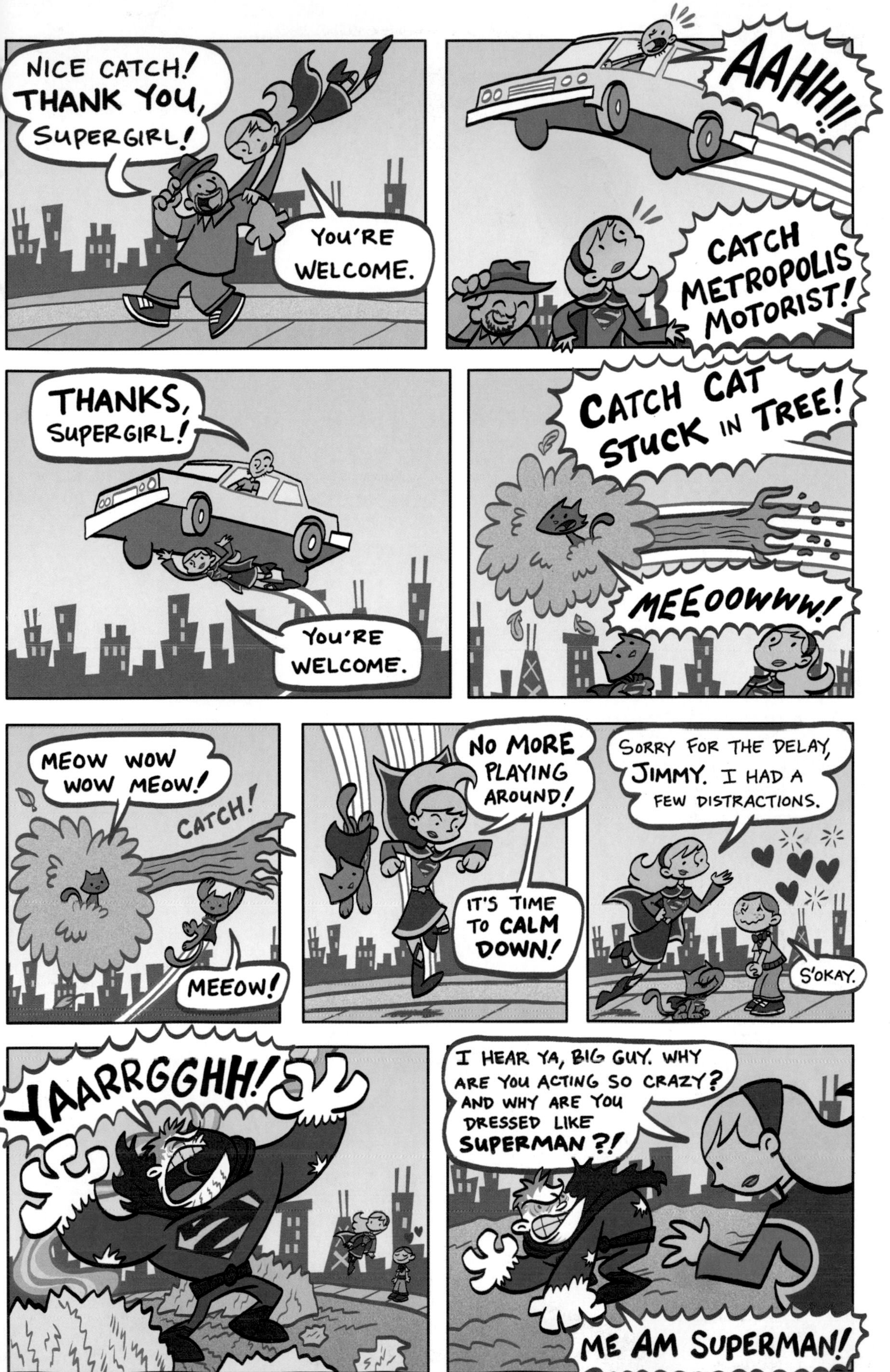
NICE CATCH! THANK YOU, SUPERGIRL!
YOU'RE WELCOME.
AAHH!!
CATCH METROPOLIS MOTORIST!
THANKS, SUPERGIRL!
YOU'RE WELCOME.
CATCH CAT STUCK IN TREE!
MEEOOWWW!
MEOW WOW WOW MEOW!
CATCH!
MEEOW!
NO MORE PLAYING AROUND!
IT'S TIME TO CALM DOWN!
SORRY FOR THE DELAY, JIMMY. I HAD A FEW DISTRACTIONS.
S'OKAY.
YAARRGGHH!
I HEAR YA, BIG GUY. WHY ARE YOU ACTING SO CRAZY? AND WHY ARE YOU DRESSED LIKE SUPERMAN?!
ME AM SUPERMAN!

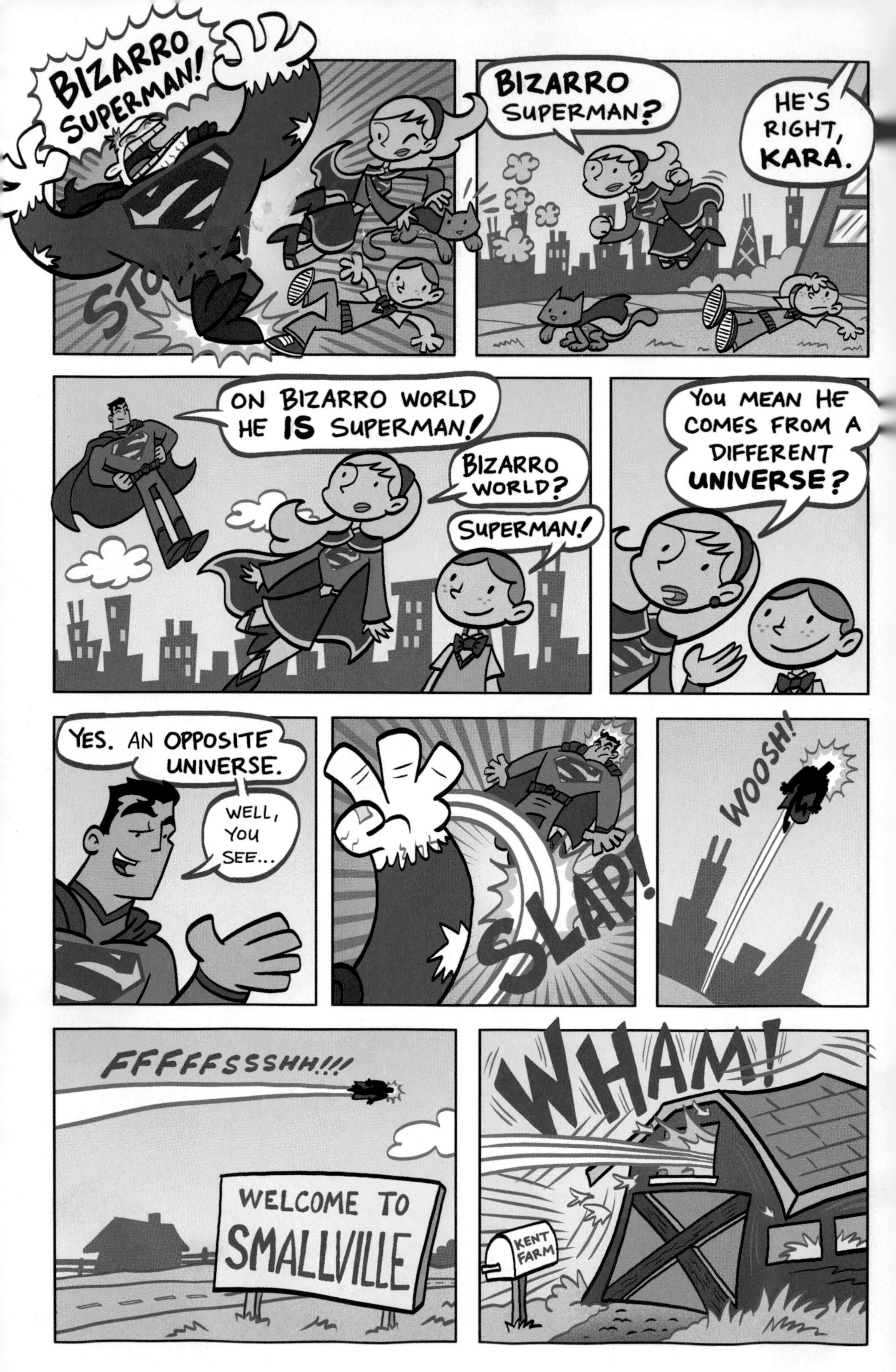

BIZARRO SUPERMAN!
STOMP!
BIZARRO SUPERMAN?
HE'S RIGHT, KARA.
ON BIZARRO WORLD HE IS SUPERMAN!
BIZARRO WORLD?
SUPERMAN!
YOU MEAN HE COMES FROM A DIFFERENT UNIVERSE?
YES. AN OPPOSITE UNIVERSE.
WELL, YOU SEE...
SLAP!
WOOSH!
FFFFFSSSHH!!!
WELCOME TO SMALLVILLE
WHAM!
KENT FARM

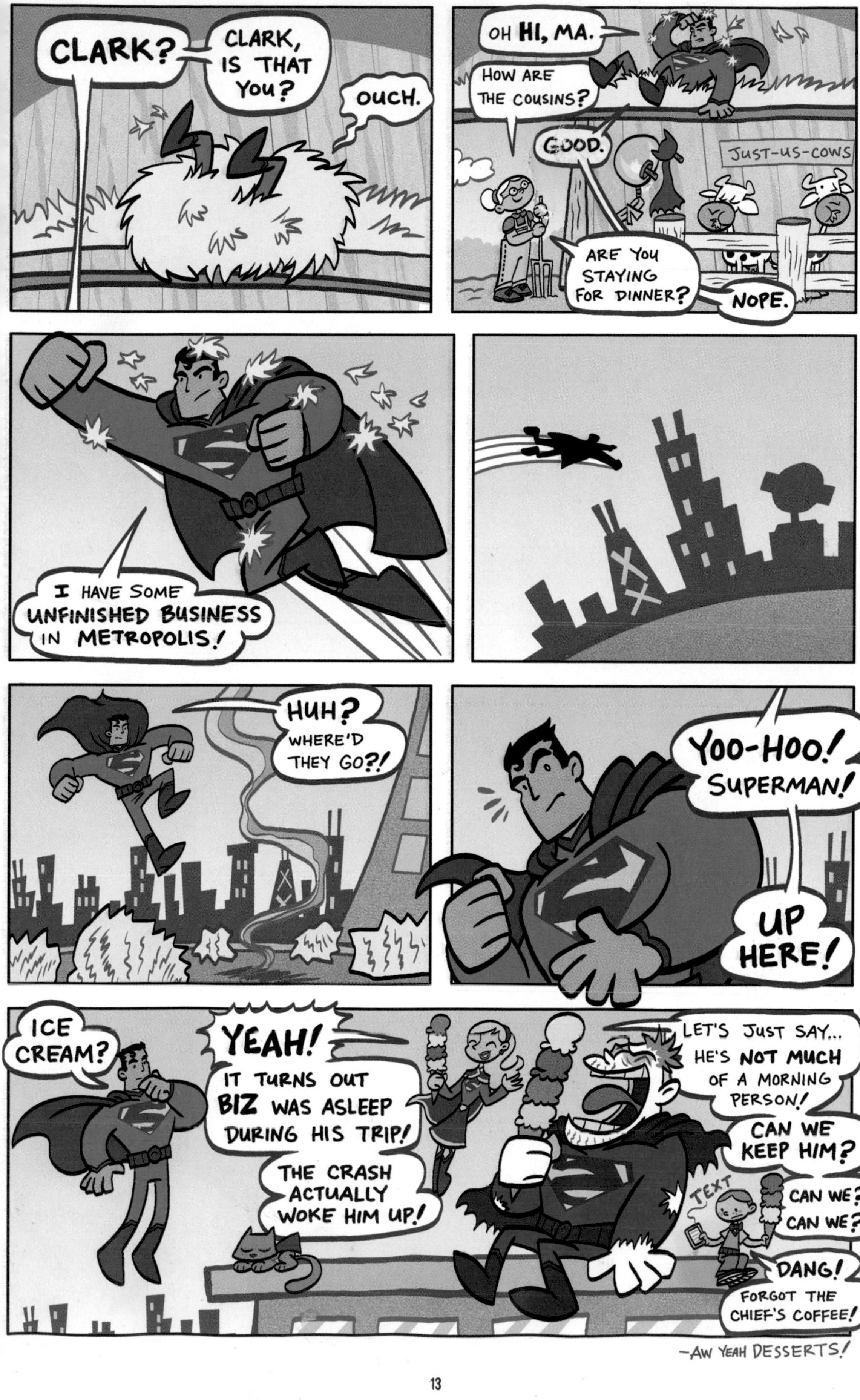
CLARK?
CLARK, IS THAT YOU?
OUCH.
OH HI, MA.
HOW ARE THE COUSINS?
GOOD.
JUST-US-COWS
ARE YOU STAYING FOR DINNER?
NOPE.
I HAVE SOME UNFINISHED BUSINESS IN METROPOLIS!
HUH? WHERE'D THEY GO?!
YOO-HOO! SUPERMAN!
UP HERE!
ICE CREAM?
YEAH! IT TURNS OUT BIZ WAS ASLEEP DURING HIS TRIP!
THE CRASH ACTUALLY WOKE HIM UP!
LET'S JUST SAY... HE'S NOT MUCH OF A MORNING PERSON!
CAN WE KEEP HIM?
TEXT
CAN WE? CAN WE?
DANG! FORGOT THE CHIEF'S COFFEE!

–AW YEAH DESSERTS!

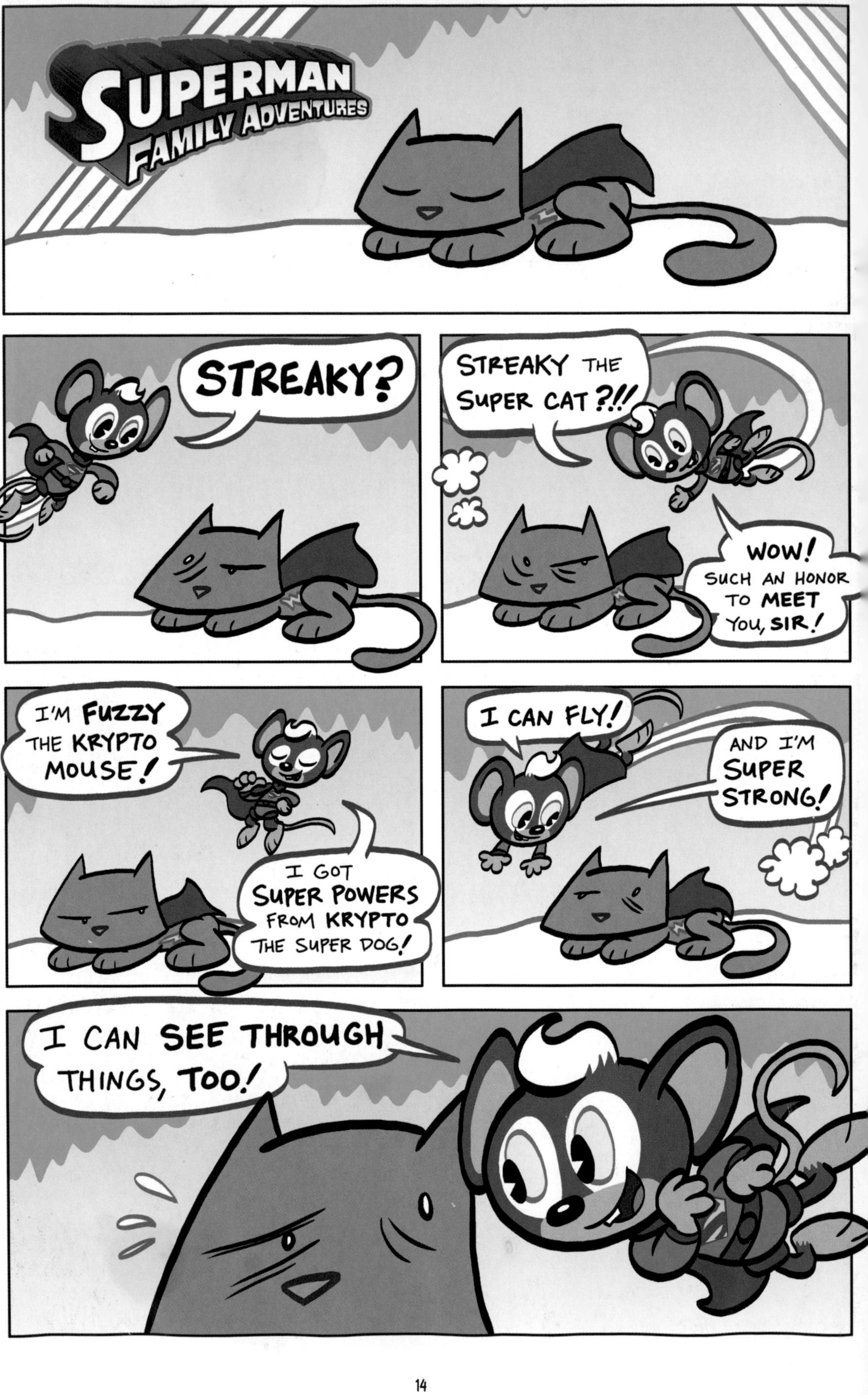
SUPERMAN FAMILY ADVENTURES
STREAKY?
STREAKY THE SUPER CAT?!!
WOW! SUCH AN HONOR TO MEET YOU, SIR!
I'M FUZZY THE KRYPTO MOUSE!
I GOT SUPER POWERS FROM KRYPTO THE SUPER DOG!
I CAN FLY!
AND I'M SUPER STRONG!
I CAN SEE THROUGH THINGS, TOO!

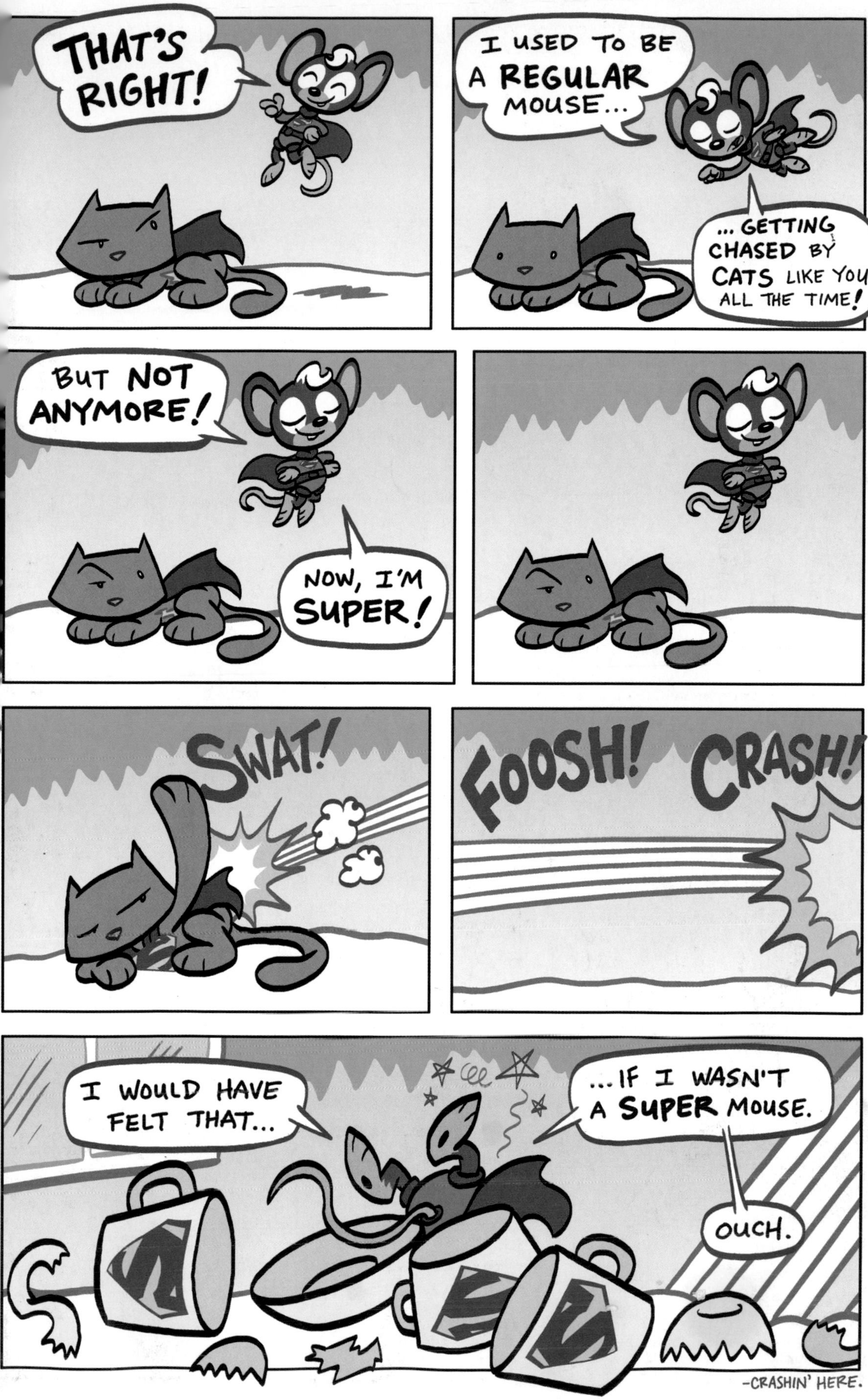
THAT'S RIGHT!
I USED TO BE A REGULAR MOUSE...
... GETTING CHASED BY CATS LIKE YOU ALL THE TIME!
BUT NOT ANYMORE!
NOW, I'M SUPER!
SWAT!
FOOSH! CRASH!
I WOULD HAVE FELT THAT...
...IF I WASN'T A SUPER MOUSE.
OUCH.

-CRASHIN' HERE.

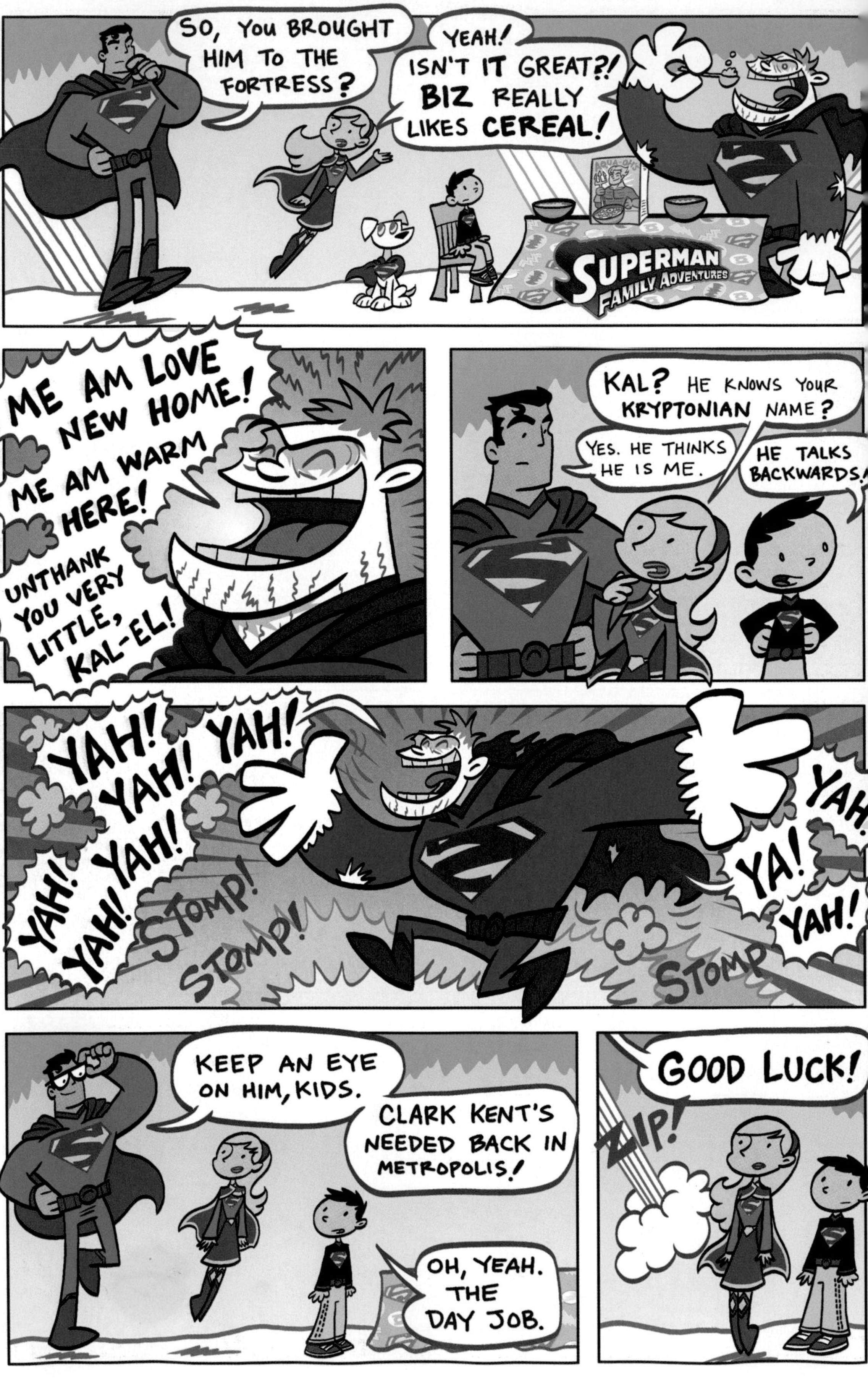
SO, YOU BROUGHT HIM TO THE FORTRESS?
YEAH! ISN'T IT GREAT?! BIZ REALLY LIKES CEREAL!
AQUA-OHS
SUPERMAN FAMILY ADVENTURES
ME AM LOVE NEW HOME!
ME AM WARM HERE!
UNTHANK YOU VERY LITTLE, KAL-EL!
KAL? HE KNOWS YOUR KRYPTONIAN NAME?
YES. HE THINKS HE IS ME.
HE TALKS BACKWARDS!
YAH! YAH! YAH! YAH! YAH! YAH! YAH!
STOMP! STOMP! STOMP
YAH! YA! YAH!
KEEP AN EYE ON HIM, KIDS.
CLARK KENT'S NEEDED BACK IN METROPOLIS!
OH, YEAH. THE DAY JOB.
GOOD LUCK!
ZIP!

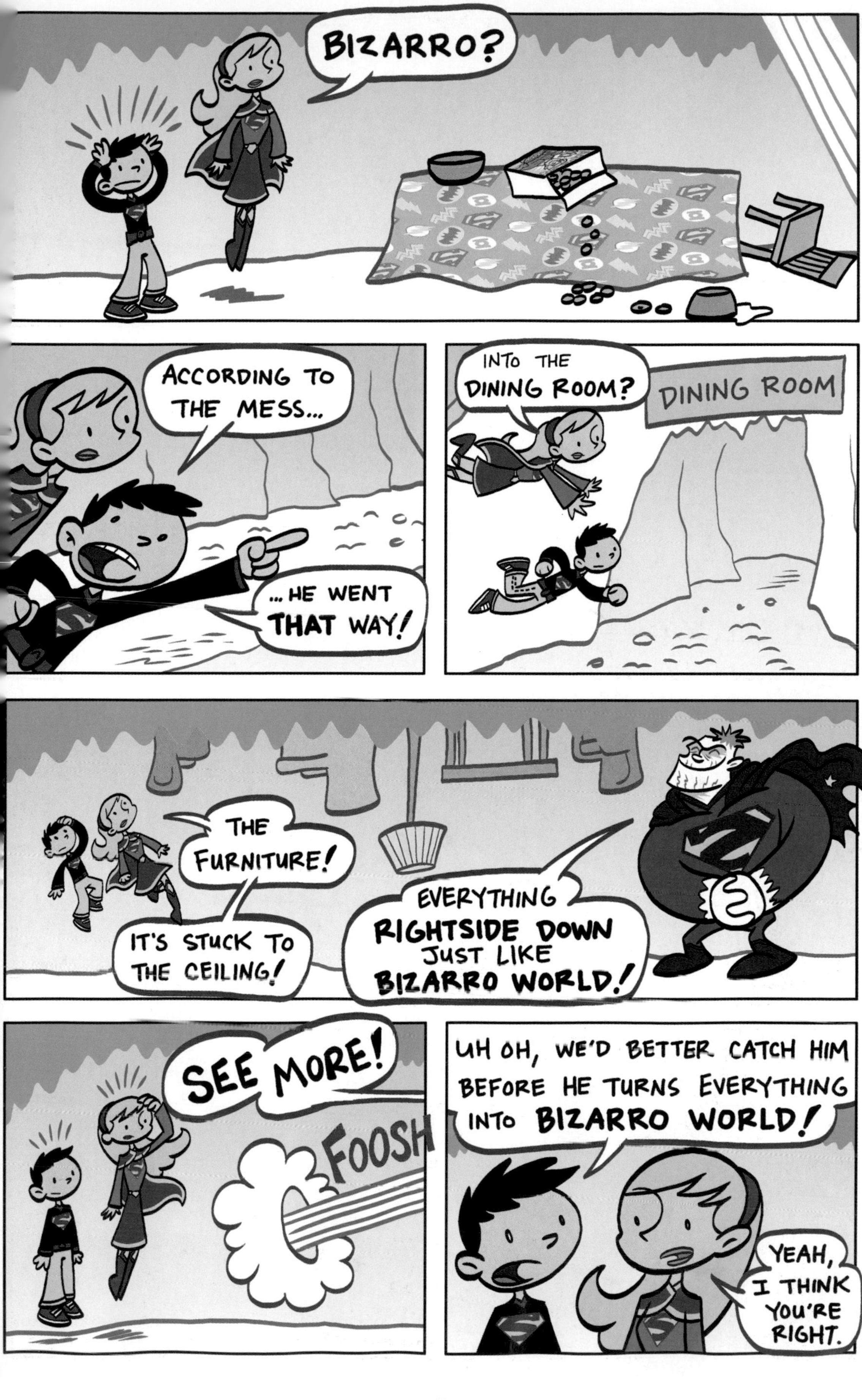
BIZARRO?
ACCORDING TO THE MESS...
...HE WENT THAT WAY!
INTO THE DINING ROOM?
DINING ROOM
THE FURNITURE!
IT'S STUCK TO THE CEILING!
EVERYTHING RIGHTSIDE DOWN JUST LIKE BIZARRO WORLD!
SEE MORE!
FOOSH
UH OH, WE'D BETTER CATCH HIM BEFORE HE TURNS EVERYTHING INTO BIZARRO WORLD!
YEAH, I THINK YOU'RE RIGHT.

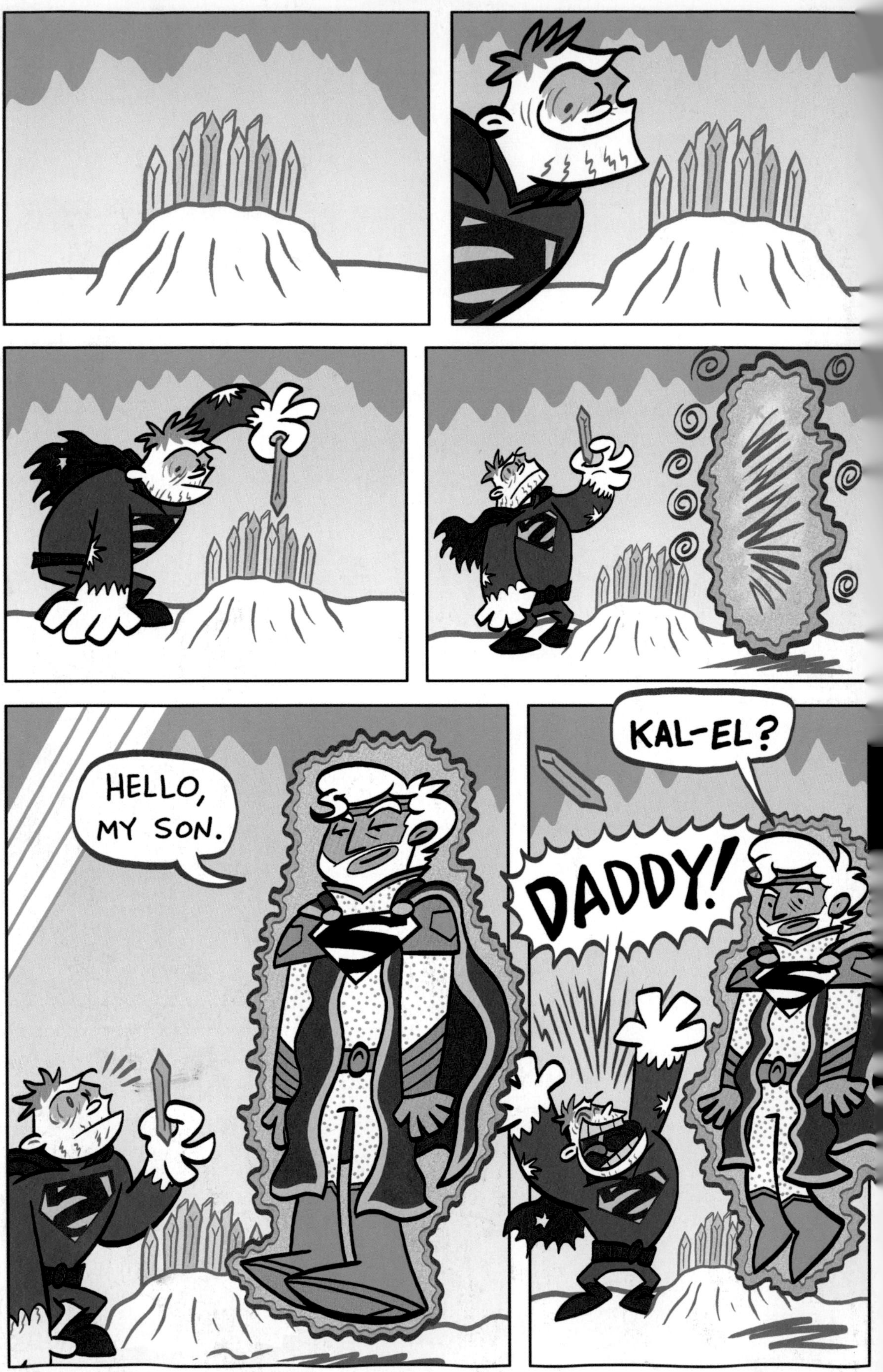
HELLO, MY SON.
KAL-EL?
DADDY!

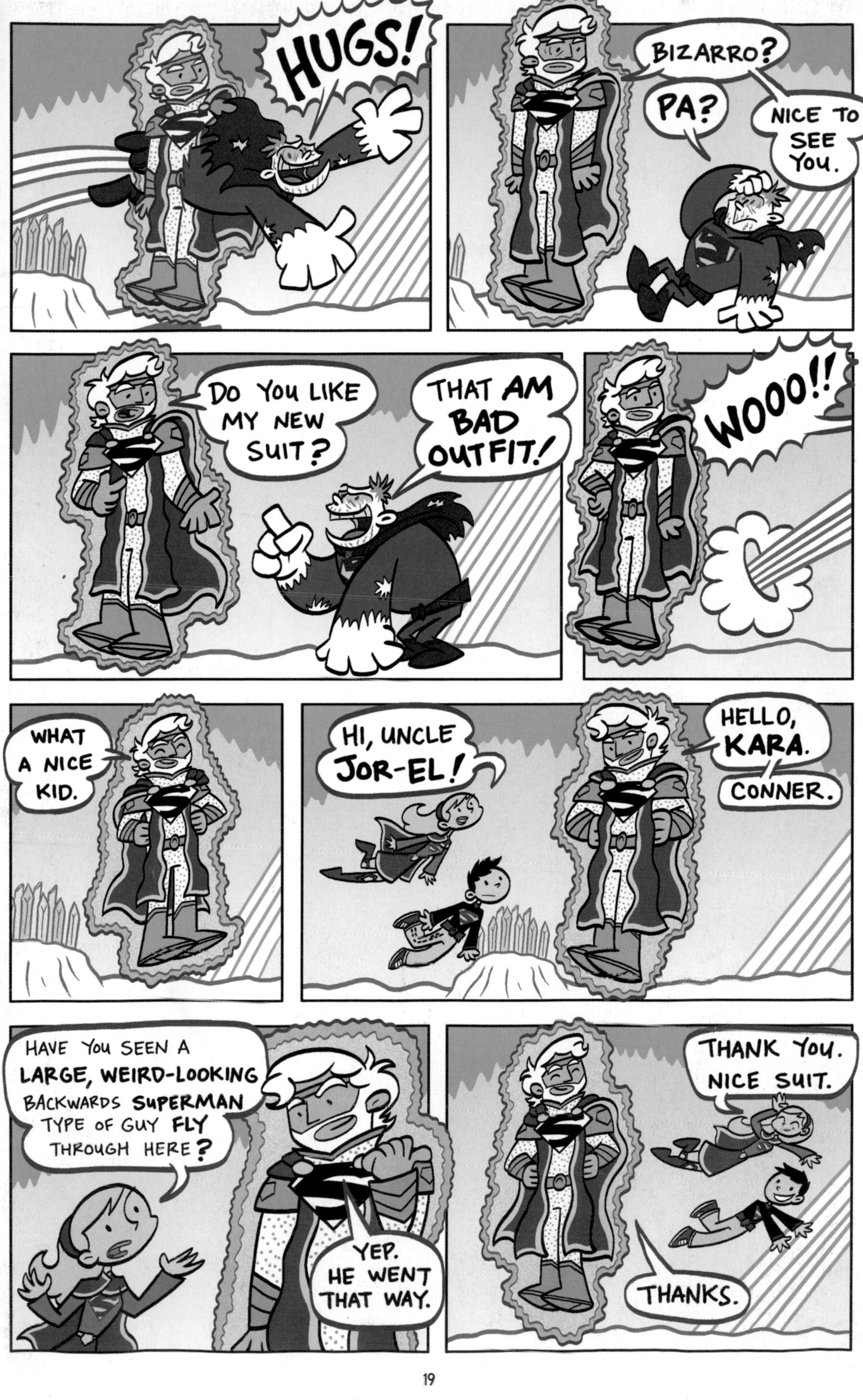
HUGS!
BIZARRO?
PA?
NICE TO SEE YOU.
DO YOU LIKE MY NEW SUIT?
THAT **AM** BAD OUTFIT!
WOOO!!
WHAT A NICE KID.
HI, UNCLE JOR-EL!
HELLO, KARA.
CONNER.
HAVE YOU SEEN A **LARGE, WEIRD-LOOKING** BACKWARDS **SUPERMAN** TYPE OF GUY **FLY** THROUGH HERE?
YEP. HE WENT THAT WAY.
THANK YOU. NICE SUIT.
THANKS.

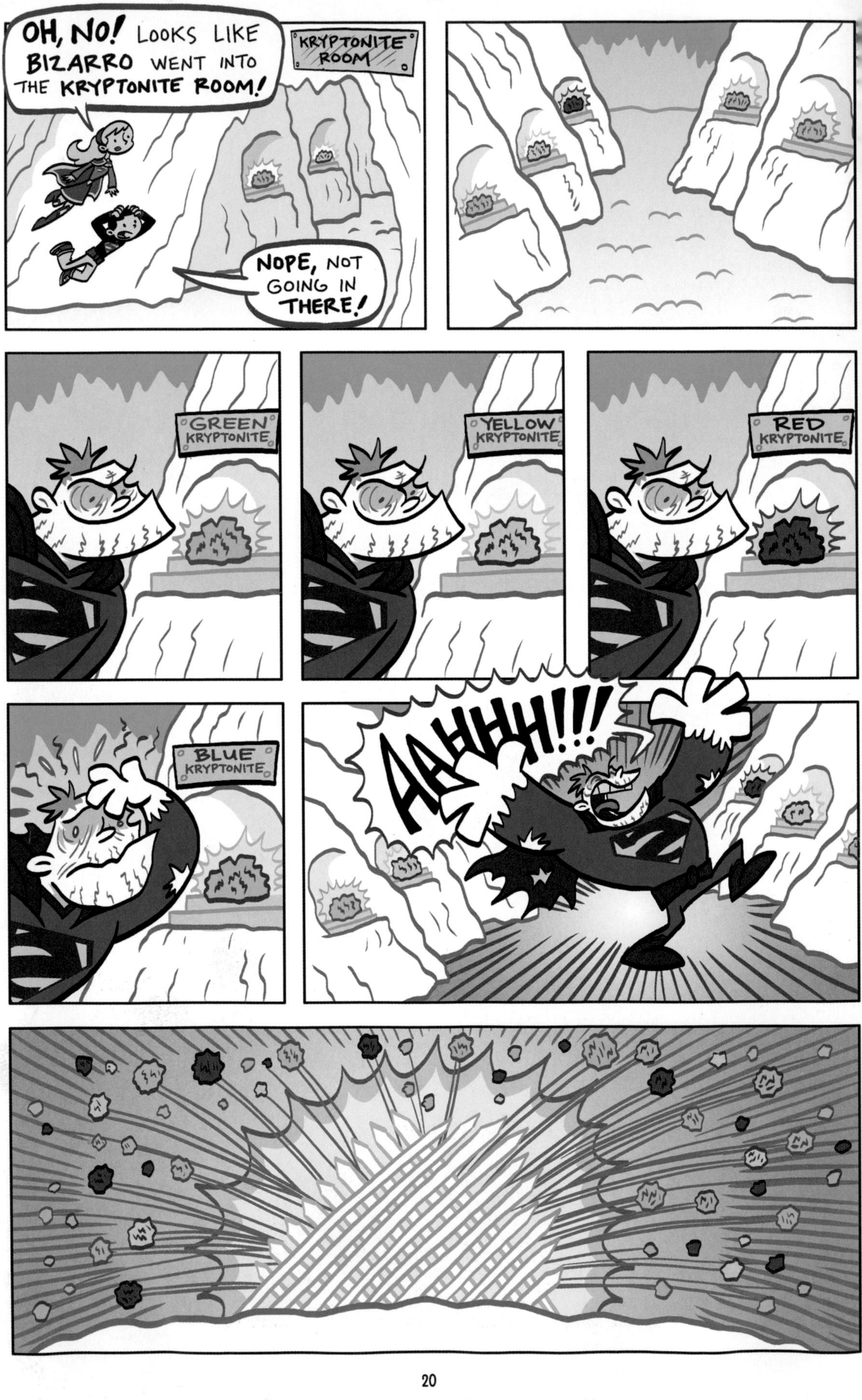
OH, NO! LOOKS LIKE BIZARRO WENT INTO THE KRYPTONITE ROOM!
KRYPTONITE ROOM
NOPE, NOT GOING IN THERE!
GREEN KRYPTONITE
YELLOW KRYPTONITE
RED KRYPTONITE
BLUE KRYPTONITE
AAHHHH!!!

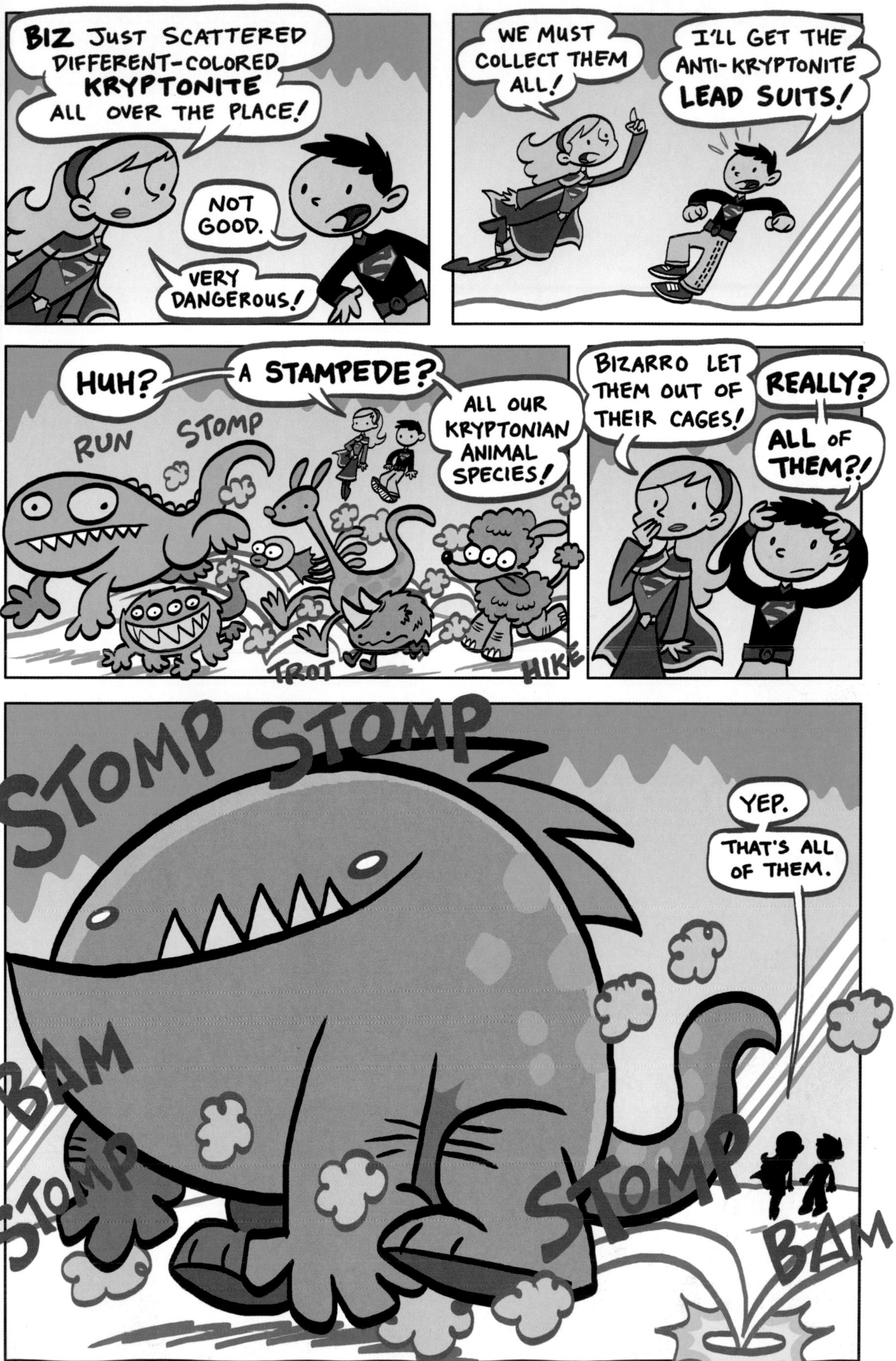
BIZ JUST SCATTERED DIFFERENT-COLORED KRYPTONITE ALL OVER THE PLACE!
NOT GOOD.
VERY DANGEROUS!
WE MUST COLLECT THEM ALL!
I'LL GET THE ANTI-KRYPTONITE LEAD SUITS!
HUH?
A STAMPEDE?
ALL OUR KRYPTONIAN ANIMAL SPECIES!
RUN
STOMP
TROT
HIKE
BIZARRO LET THEM OUT OF THEIR CAGES!
REALLY?
ALL OF THEM?!
STOMP STOMP
YEP.
THAT'S ALL OF THEM.
BAM
STOMP
STOMP
BAM

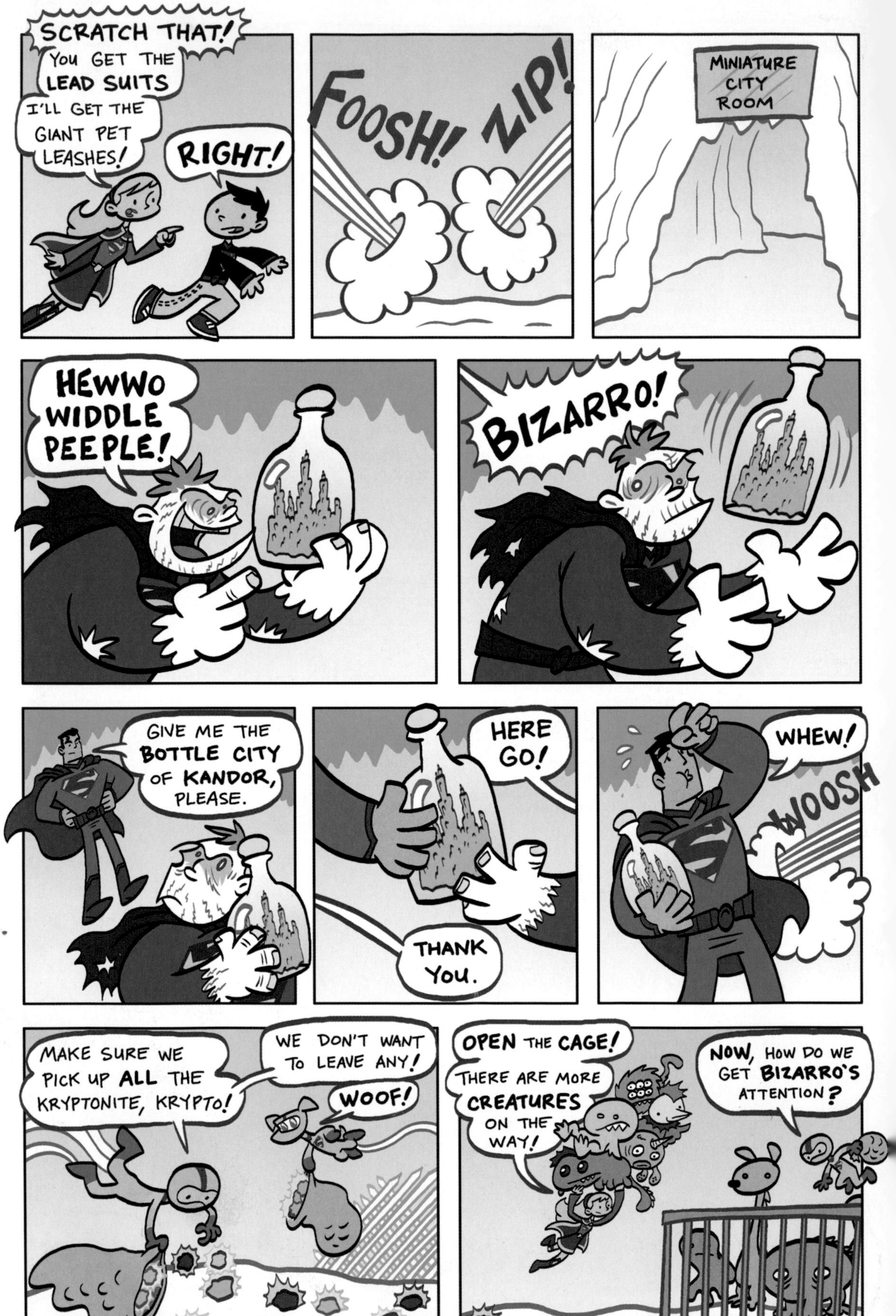
SCRATCH THAT!
YOU GET THE LEAD SUITS
I'LL GET THE GIANT PET LEASHES!
RIGHT!
FOOSH!
ZIP!
MINIATURE CITY ROOM
HEWWO WIDDLE PEEPLE!
BIZARRO!
GIVE ME THE BOTTLE CITY OF KANDOR, PLEASE.
HERE GO!
THANK YOU.
WHEW!
WOOSH
MAKE SURE WE PICK UP ALL THE KRYPTONITE, KRYPTO!
WE DON'T WANT TO LEAVE ANY!
WOOF!
OPEN THE CAGE!
THERE ARE MORE CREATURES ON THE WAY!
NOW, HOW DO WE GET BIZARRO'S ATTENTION?

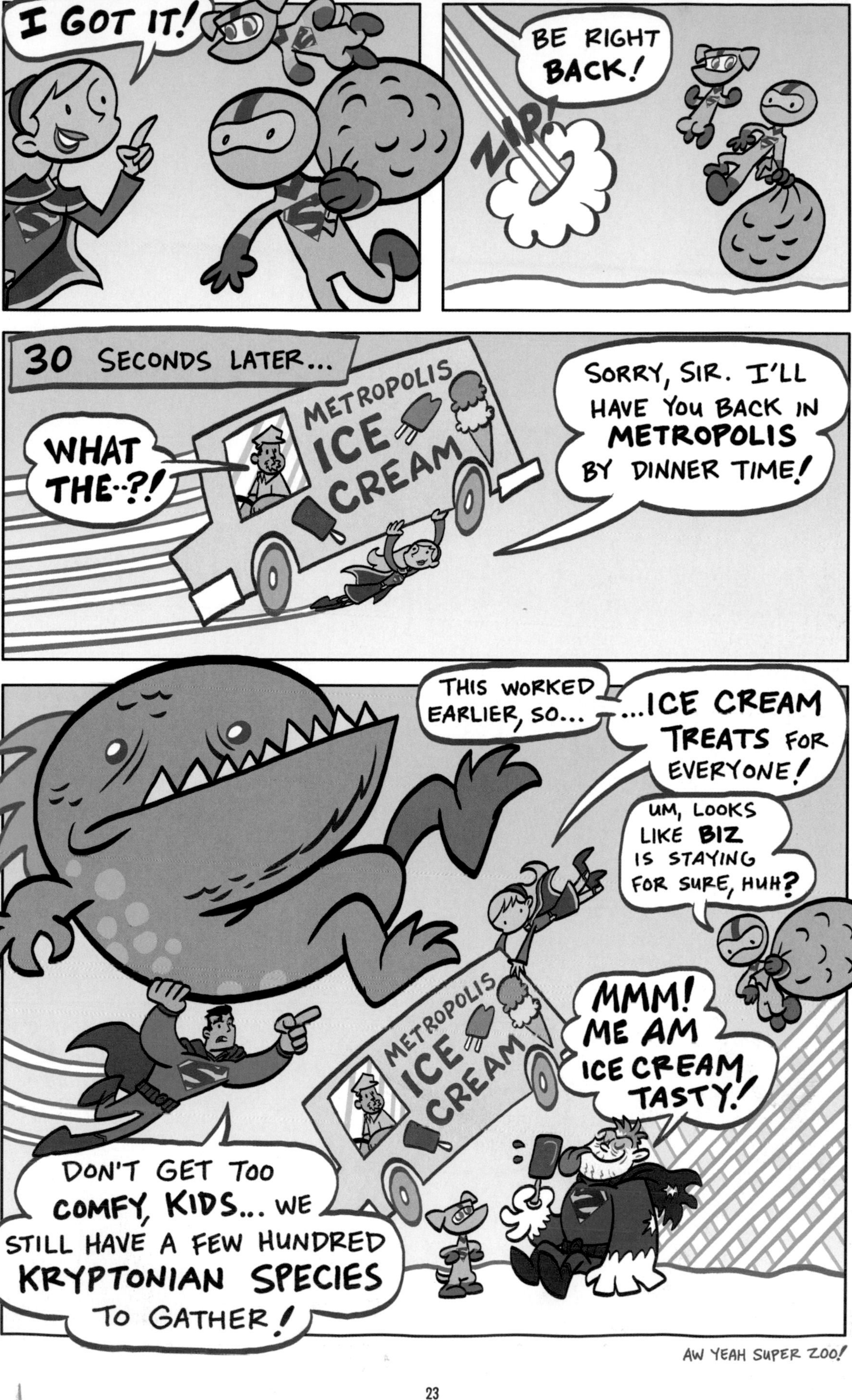
I GOT IT!
BE RIGHT BACK!
ZIP!
30 SECONDS LATER...
METROPOLIS ICE CREAM
WHAT THE..?!
SORRY, SIR. I'LL HAVE YOU BACK IN METROPOLIS BY DINNER TIME!
THIS WORKED EARLIER, SO...
...ICE CREAM TREATS FOR EVERYONE!
UM, LOOKS LIKE BIZ IS STAYING FOR SURE, HUH?
METROPOLIS ICE CREAM
MMM! ME AM ICE CREAM TASTY!
DON'T GET TOO COMFY, KIDS... WE STILL HAVE A FEW HUNDRED KRYPTONIAN SPECIES TO GATHER!

AW YEAH SUPER ZOO!

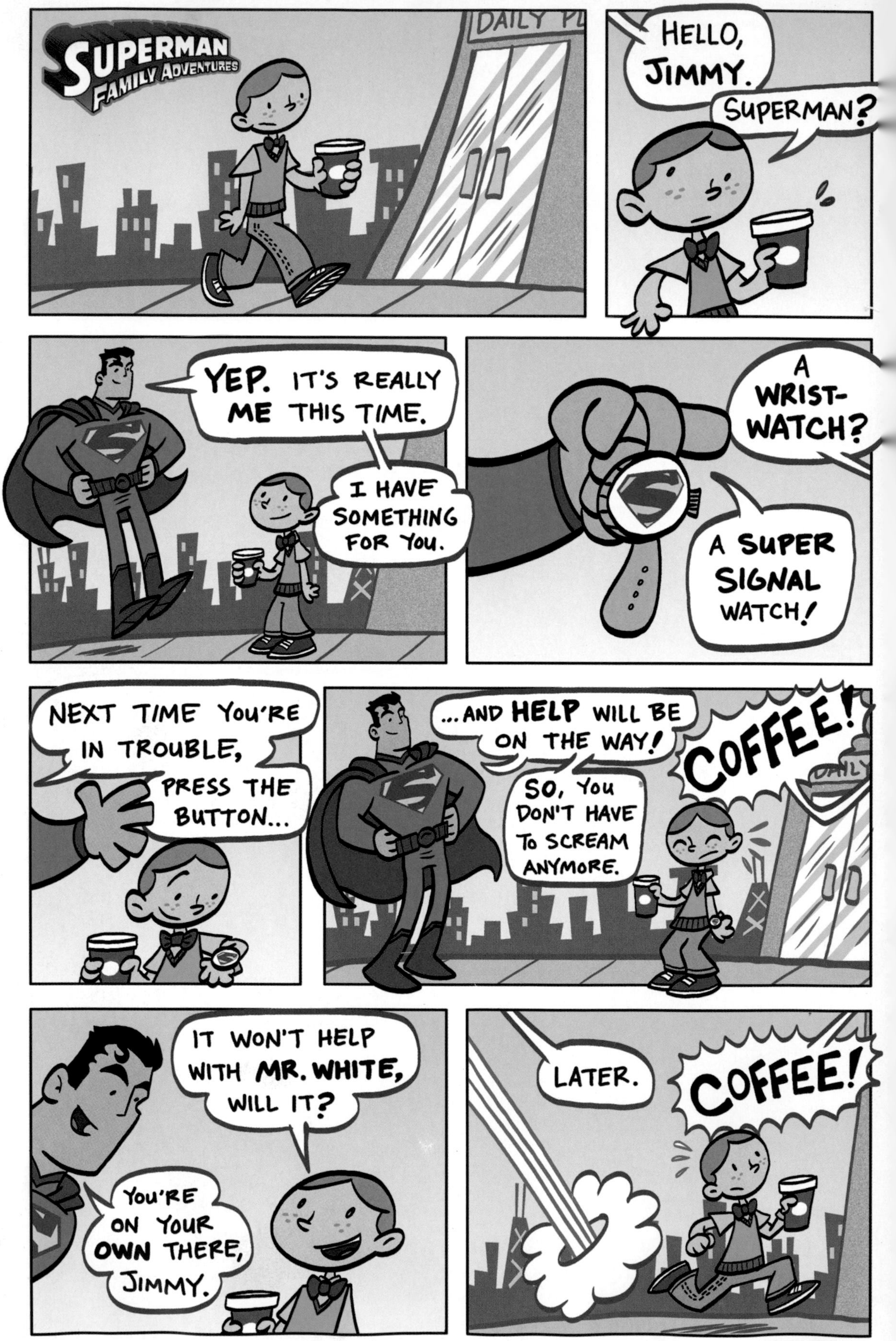
SUPERMAN FAMILY ADVENTURES
DAILY PL
HELLO, JIMMY.
SUPERMAN?
YEP. IT'S REALLY ME THIS TIME.
I HAVE SOMETHING FOR YOU.
A WRIST-WATCH?
A SUPER SIGNAL WATCH!
NEXT TIME YOU'RE IN TROUBLE,
PRESS THE BUTTON...
...AND HELP WILL BE ON THE WAY!
SO, YOU DON'T HAVE TO SCREAM ANYMORE.
COFFEE!
DAILY
IT WON'T HELP WITH MR. WHITE, WILL IT?
YOU'RE ON YOUR OWN THERE, JIMMY.
LATER.
COFFEE!
-YES, SIR!

SUPERMAN®
FAMILY ADVENTURES™

CREATORS

ART BALTAZAR IS A CARTOONIST MACHINE FROM THE HEART OF CHICAGO! HE DEFINES CARTOONS AND COMICS NOT ONLY AS AN ART STYLE, BUT AS A WAY OF LIFE. CURRENTLY, ART IS THE CREATIVE FORCE BEHIND THE NEW YORK TIMES BEST-SELLING, EISNER AWARD-WINNING, DC COMICS SERIES TINY TITANS, AND THE CO-WRITER FOR BILLY BATSON AND THE MAGIC OF SHAZAM! AND CO-CREATOR OF SUPERMAN FAMILY ADVENTURES. ART IS LIVING THE DREAM! HE DRAWS COMICS AND NEVER HAS TO LEAVE THE HOUSE. HE LIVES WITH HIS LOVELY WIFE, ROSE, BIG BOY SONNY, LITTLE BOY GORDON, AND LITTLE GIRL AUDREY. RIGHT ON!

ART BALTAZAR

FRANCO

FRANCO AURELIANI, BRONX, NEW YORK BORN WRITER AND ARTIST, HAS BEEN DRAWING COMICS SINCE HE COULD HOLD A CRAYON. CURRENTLY RESIDING IN UPSTATE NEW YORK WITH HIS WIFE, IVETTE, AND SON, NICOLAS, FRANCO SPENDS MOST OF HIS DAYS IN A BATCAVE-LIKE STUDIO WHERE HE PRODUCES DC'S TINY TITANS COMICS. IN 1995, FRANCO FOUNDED BLINDWOLF STUDIOS, AN INDEPENDENT ART STUDIO WHERE HE AND FELLOW CREATORS CAN CREATE CHILDREN'S COMICS. FRANCO IS THE CREATOR, ARTIST, AND WRITER OF WEIRDSVILLE, L'IL CREEPS, AND EAGLE ALL STAR, AS WELL AS THE CO-CREATOR AND WRITER OF PATRICK THE WOLF BOY. WHEN HE'S NOT WRITING AND DRAWING, FRANCO ALSO TEACHES HIGH SCHOOL ART.

GLOSSARY

attention (uh-TEN-shuhn)– careful listening or watching

collision (kuh-LIZH-uhn)–the act or instance of crashing together forcefully, often at high speeds

comfy (KUHM-fee)–comfortable, or allowing relaxation or the feeling of pleasure

distraction (diss-TRAKT-shuhn)–something that makes it hard to pay attention

fortress (FOR-triss)–a place that is strengthened against attack

lead (LED)–a soft, gray metal

meteor (MEE-tee-ur)–a piece of rock or metal from space that enters Earth's atmosphere at high speeds, burns, and forms a streak of light as it falls to Earth

motorist (MOH-tur-ist)–someone who travels by car

opposite (OP-uh-zit)–a person, thing, or idea that is completely different from another

stampede (stam-PEED)–a sudden, wild rush in one direction, usually because something has been frightened

universe (YOO-nuh-vurss)–the earth, the planet, the stars, and all things that exist in space

VISUAL QUESTIONS & PROMPTS

1. BIZARRO IS THE EXACT OPPOSITE OF SUPERMAN. GO BACK THROUGH THE STORY AND FIND AT LEAST TWO THINGS THAT MAKE HIM DIFFERENT FROM THE MAN OF STEEL.

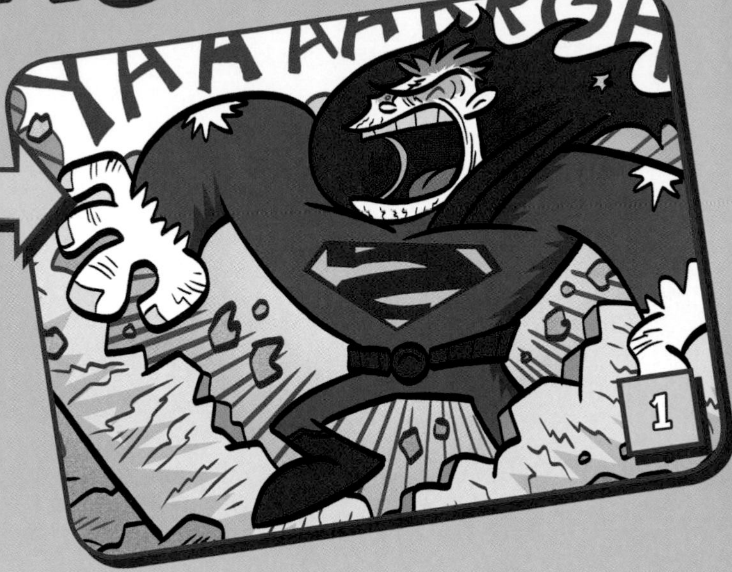
1

2. IN COMIC BOOKS, AN ILLUSTRATOR SOMETIMES DRAWS OBJECTS OR SHAPES ABOVE A CHARACTER'S HEAD TO SHOW HOW HE OR SHE IS FEELING. HOW DO YOU THINK JIMMY IS FEELING IN THE PANEL AT RIGHT?

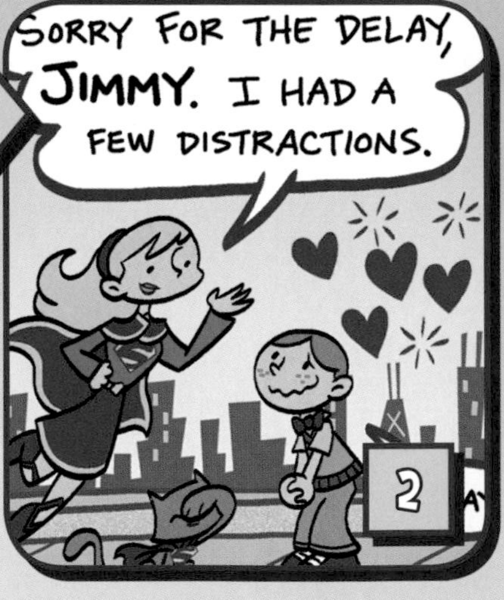
SORRY FOR THE DELAY, JIMMY. I HAD A FEW DISTRACTIONS.
2

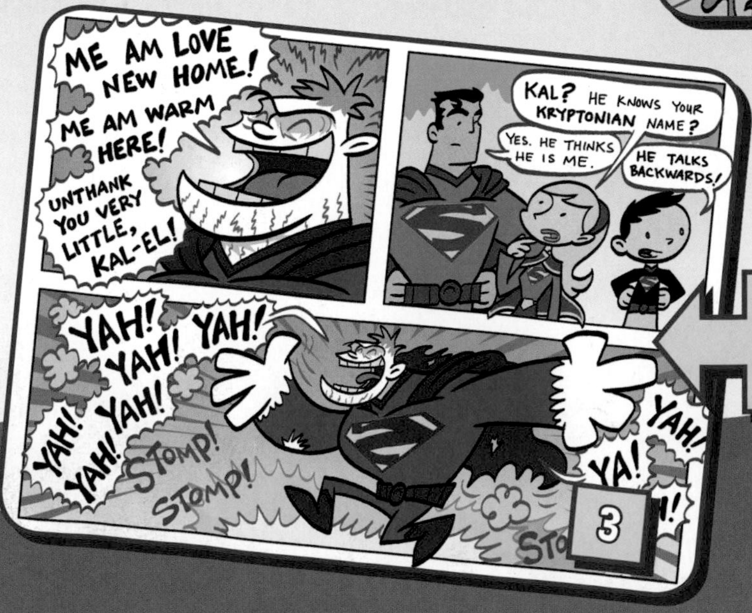
ME AM LOVE NEW HOME!
ME AM WARM HERE!
UNTHANK YOU VERY LITTLE, KAL-EL!
KAL? HE KNOWS YOUR KRYPTONIAN NAME?
YES. HE THINKS HE IS ME.
HE TALKS BACKWARDS!
YAH! YAH! YAH! YAH! YAH! YAH!
STOMP! STOMP!
YAH! YA!
3

3. DO YOU THINK BIZARRO IS A BAD GUY OR A GOOD GUY? EXPLAIN YOUR ANSWER USING EXAMPLES FROM THE STORY.

GREEN KRYPTONITE
KRYPTONITE
KRYPTONITE

BLUE KRYPTONITE
4

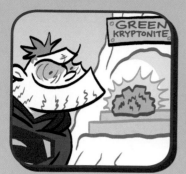

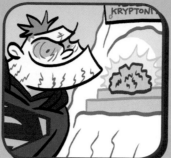

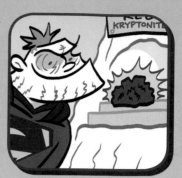

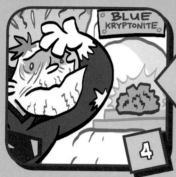

4. THERE ARE MANY DIFFERENT COLORS OF KRYPTONITE. THE GREEN KRYPTONITE DRAINS SUPERMAN'S POWERS. WHAT DO YOU THINK THE OTHER COLORS DO?

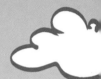

5. DRAW YOUR OWN KRYPTONIAN SPECIES! MAKE THEM COLORFUL, FUN, AND GIVE THEM ALL NAMES.

E ARE MORE
EATURES
N THE
WAY!
NOW, HOW DO WE GET BIZARRO'S ATTENTION?
5

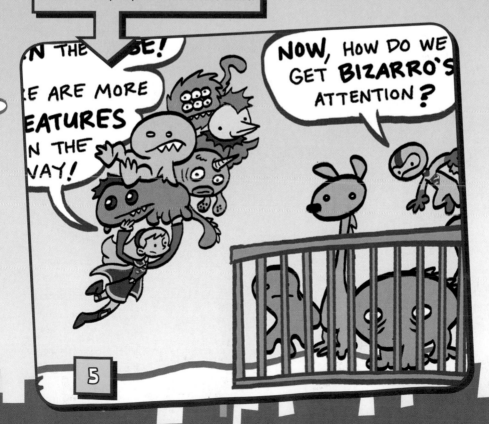

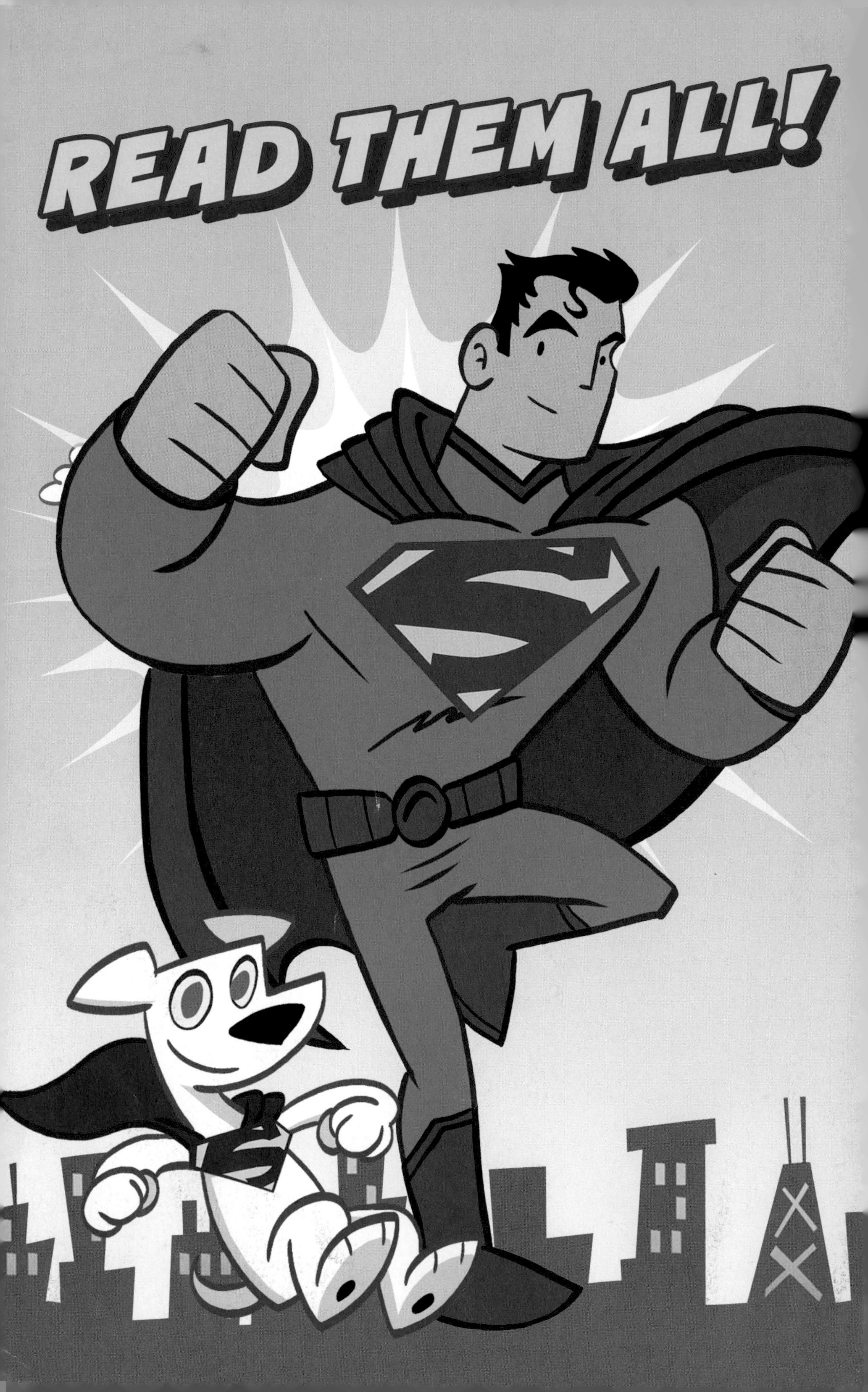
READ THEM ALL!

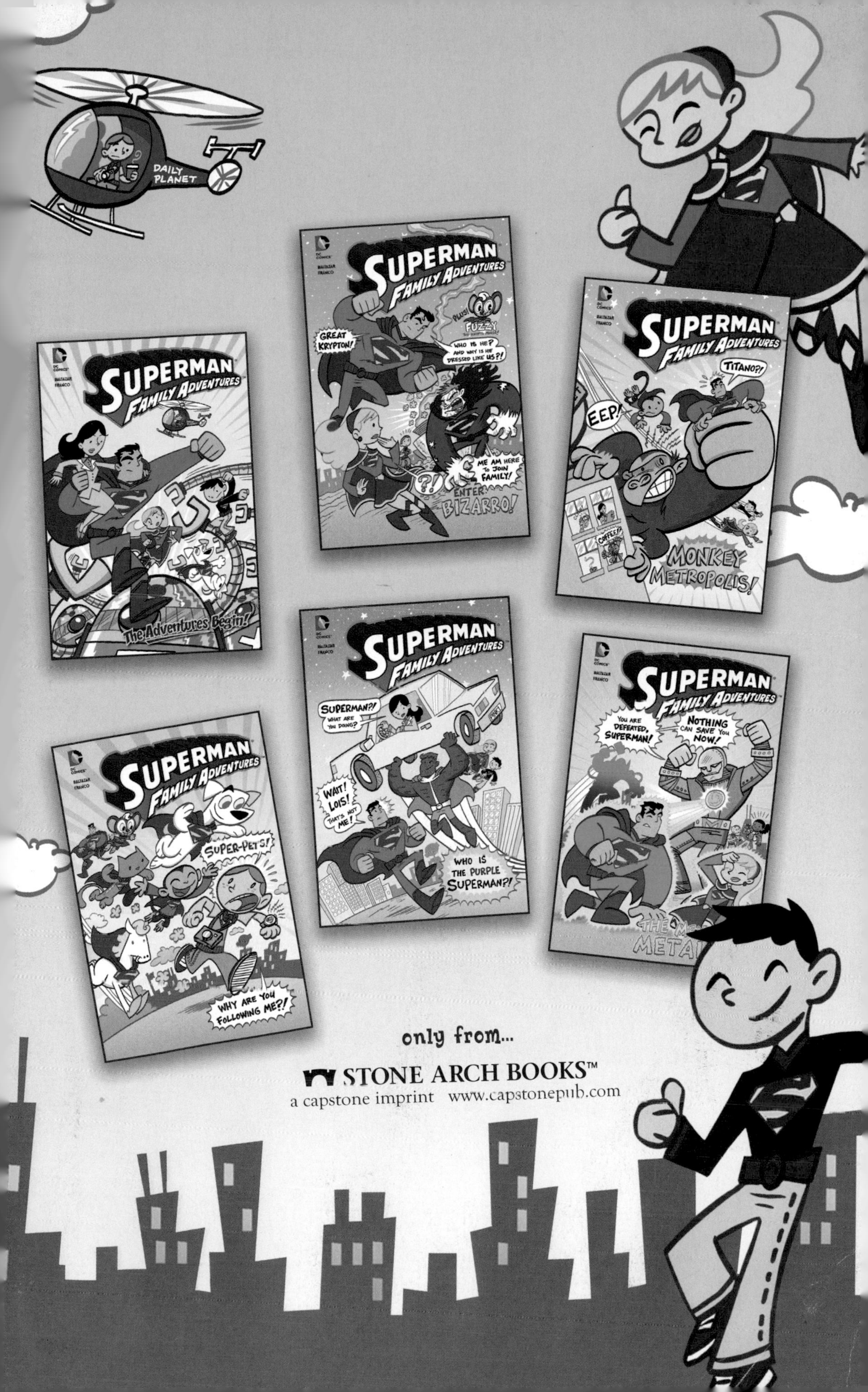
DAILY PLANET
SUPERMAN FAMILY ADVENTURES
The Adventures Begin!
SUPERMAN FAMILY ADVENTURES
GREAT KRYPTON!
WHO IS HE? AND WHY IS HE DRESSED LIKE US?!
ME AM HERE TO JOIN FAMILY!
?!
ENTER: BIZARRO!
SUPERMAN FAMILY ADVENTURES
TITANO?!
EEP!
COFFEE!?
MONKEY METROPOLIS!
SUPERMAN FAMILY ADVENTURES
SUPER-PETS!
WHY ARE YOU FOLLOWING ME?!
SUPERMAN FAMILY ADVENTURES
SUPERMAN?! WHAT ARE YOU DOING?
WAIT! LOIS! THAT'S NOT ME!
WHO IS THE PURPLE SUPERMAN?!
SUPERMAN FAMILY ADVENTURES
YOU ARE DEFEATED, SUPERMAN!
NOTHING CAN SAVE YOU NOW!
only from...
STONE ARCH BOOKS™
a capstone imprint www.capstonepub.com

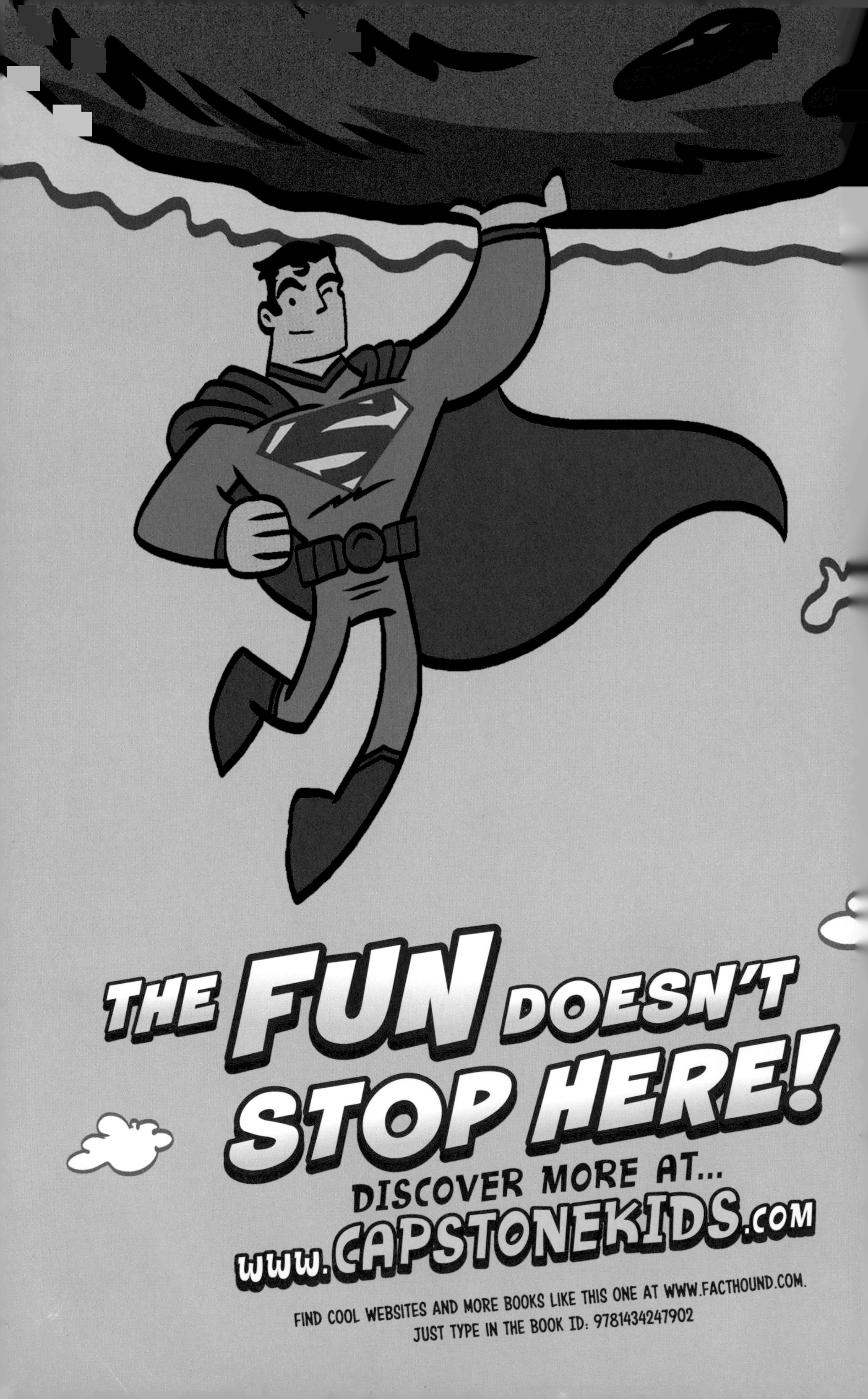
THE FUN DOESN'T STOP HERE!
DISCOVER MORE AT...
WWW.CAPSTONEKIDS.COM
FIND COOL WEBSITES AND MORE BOOKS LIKE THIS ONE AT WWW.FACTHOUND.COM.
JUST TYPE IN THE BOOK ID: 9781434247902